The Dragon Clock

Andrew is fascinated by his grandmother's
Dragon Clock – and just a little bit afraid of it.
One night the figures on the clock come to
life, and Andrew is launched into an amazing
adventure as he tries to help his friend
Princess Plumpearl in her desperate struggle
against the cruel Ice Sorcerer from the north.

Marjorie-Ann Watts was trained as a
painter and illustrator but now spends most
of her time writing her own stories for
children. She is married, has two sons, and is
the author and illustrator of *The Mill House
Cat*, which is also published by Beaver.

THE DRAGON CLOCK

Written and illustrated by
Marjorie-Ann Watts

Beaver Books

A Beaver Book
Published by Arrow Books Limited
17-21 Conway Street, London W1P 6JD
An imprint of the Hutchinson Publishing Group
London Melbourne Sydney Auckland Johannesburg
and agencies throughout the world

First published in 1974 by
David & Charles Limited
Beaver edition 1984
© Copyright text and illustrations Marjorie-Ann Watts 1974 and 1984

Set in Baskerville
Printed and bound in Great Britain by
Anchor Brendon Limited, Tiptree, Essex

ISBN 0 09 933820 3

Contents

For my Mother

1 *The Dragon Clock*

Andrew's grandmother, Mrs Jamieson, lived in a tall house set back in a shabby street just off the Bayswater Road. Andrew loved everything about Verbena Lodge, as it was called, and came to stay quite often. Not only was it unlike any other house he'd visited, but there were so many interesting things to see and do in it, that he felt he would never have time for them all; and people didn't seem to bother him there the way they did at home: 'Clean your teeth, wipe your feet, do this! do that!' On and on and on, all day long. When he was on a visit to Verbena Lodge, he could spend the day as he pleased – well, almost.

Best of all, perhaps was his grandmother's collection of clocks. Not counting the three grandfather clocks that stood in the hall, there were eighty-six different clocks crammed into the two big downstairs rooms alone. Goodness knows how many there were all over the rest of the house. Hundreds probably.

Andrew wound most of the clocks downstairs, and some of the ones upstairs, but there was one he always left to his grandmother, and that was a fairly recent arrival, the huge lacquered wall clock that hung on the upstairs landing. He could not explain why, but he preferred her to deal with that, although he always watched while it was wound. 'The Dragon Clock', Mrs Jamieson called it; this

7

was because of the two ornately carved dragons on either side of the gilded face.

Mrs Jamieson had bought it at a sale in the country. 'I couldn't find out much about it,' she said when she brought it home. 'The man said it was just dumped on him. But look at it, Andrew! In the old days people thought that this sort of clock had magical properties – and I can well believe it! I wish I knew more about it.'

Once the clock was wound, it went on ticking for half a year, keeping perfect time. 'That's on account of the dragons!' Mrs Jamieson would say smiling mysteriously. 'They make sure it tells the right time!'

Sometimes, as Andrew passed on the landing, he would stop to look at the red carved dragons on either side of the face, their teeth bared in a perpetual snarl, their round bulging eyes staring angrily out at the world. 'It would be all right if they were on your side!' he would say to himself.

On the lacquered panel below the clock face, a strange landscape was painted, which grew more interesting and more real to Andrew every time he studied it; he was always finding fresh things which he hadn't noticed before. There was a river, zigzagging between some rather conical hills; trees with enormous leaves like flowers; a little bridge, and in the distance, in front of a high range of mountains, a strange complicated palace, with many towers and pinnacles sticking up into the sky. There were animals running and playing beneath the trees; and on the bridge, dressed in long regal clothes, stood a figure gazing down into the water. Because of the long dress, Andrew thought it was probably a girl. He even had a name for her – Princess Plumpearl.

There was another person in the house who was interested in the Dragon Clock, and that was Scratchit, Mrs Jamieson's red and grey parrot. He was often to be seen sitting on the top, with his head twisted round, staring at the dragons below; or stalking about the upstairs landing screaming 'Hullo Darling! Marry me! Marry me!' and other ridiculous remarks at anyone who passed. Scratchit had quite a large vocabulary – although most of the time he didn't use it. Andrew sometimes wondered if he, Scratchit, could talk perfectly well, but preferred not to. 'The Frightful Fowl', Andrew's father called Scratchit; and his mother just thought it was terribly unhygienic keeping a parrot loose in the house – which it was, of course.

'Well! I can't keep him locked up all the time,' old Mrs Jamieson would say mildly – she was very fond of Scratchit – and then she would try rather half-heartedly to push the parrot into his cage. But usually he was too quick for her; and Andrew would spend many happy hours stalking Scratchit all over the house, until finally 'The Frightful Fowl' was cornered.

On this particular afternoon, Scratchit was already in his cage, and all the clocks were fully wound. Andrew pressed his nose against the cold glass, and stared out of the window. At the back of Verbena Lodge, a long narrow garden joined a lot of other long narrow gardens, in a jumble of crumbling walls, old trees, broken gates, and half seen glimpses of distant roofs. Here, where the gardens of four streets met and made the inside of a huge square, Andrew liked to be. He rode his bike along the paths; climbed the walls; explored the roofs of other people's sheds and outhouses, or climbed as high as he could into the giant chestnut, at the far end of his grandmother's garden. As long as he could remember, he had never met anyone at all in The Gardens. It was always quiet and deserted; and this was almost the best thing about it.

I think I'll go down now, he thought. The sun's come out, and I'll be able to try out my telescope. The week before, his father had given him a pocket telescope, as a late birthday present. There'll be a good view from the chestnut.

He ran down the stairs, and put on his wellingtons, as it had rained during the morning. There was nobody about. Miss Shooter, his grandmother's companion, was in the kitchen making scones and Mrs Jamieson was having a nap. He fetched his bike from the cupboard under the stairs, and rode into the drawing-room, and out through the open french windows on to the grass beyond.

The chestnut must have been hundreds of years old. An enormous tree, it stood spreading its graceful branches tier upon tier, just beside the boundary wall, potting shed on one side, compost heaps on the other.

It was almost as if it had been grown especially to be climbed. Like walking up a staircase, Andrew thought as he hoisted himself up through the branches. In a few minutes he was as high as it was safe to go, lying comfortably on a platform of broad planks that some other children had nailed up there long ago. Beneath him, the gardens lay, spread out like an irregular chessboard; and through a gap in the leaves before him, he could see the back of St Anne's Terrace, a very grand row of posh houses overlooking the park. Nearer was the roof of a house that had interested him for a long time. Only a dormer window, part of the roof and a bit of brickwork showed. The rest was hidden by the branches of the chestnut. From the ground the house couldn't be seen at all, though he was pretty sure it must be the back of Mr Grottel's shop.

Mr Grottel! Andrew frowned, took a crumpled bag of toffees from his pocket, and rolling over on to his back, lay looking up at the complicated tangle of leaves above him.

He could never quite decide about Mr Grottel. He was certainly very peculiar, although interesting to talk to;

10

and his shop was marvellous! It was called the Magic Shop, and besides being crammed to the ceiling with all the usual paraphernalia of party conjurers and magicians – loaded dice, packs of trick cards, disappearing handker-chiefs and so on – Mr Grottel specialised in second-hand jewellery and bric-à-brac, books, and antique clocks of every description. He also sold very lifelike masks which slipped right over your head; false hands with long curved nails made of rubber, and ventriloquists' dummies which sat high up on a narrow shelf at the back of the shop, scrutinising any visitor with their round desperate eyes. The shop was usually empty, although occasionally one or two customers called: men who earned their livings as professional magicians – or so Mr Grottel said.

Mostly Mr Grottel was friendly, in an odd jokey sort of way; and he would perform extraordinary tricks – making dice appear from an empty bottle, guessing a card picked at random and that sort of thing – with the greatest of ease.

'But how do you do it?' Andrew would say amazed.

'Practice!' Mr Grottel would reply, adding in a whisper, 'and Magic! Don't you believe in magic?'

'Er-yes! Well – a bit,' Andrew had said. 'Yes, I suppose I do. Sometimes.'

'A Sorcerer's Apprentice – eh?' Mr Grottel started to laugh quietly in his peculiar way. 'I could show you things – that – would ASTONISH you!' and he bent over the counter and stared very hard at Andrew. But at that moment, the little bell on top of the door tinkled, and a rare customer appeared; so Andrew had left to get the bread from the dairy opposite, which was what he was supposed to be doing.

Stacked against the glass counter at the side were some boxes, one of which you could get into, and pretend to be sawn in half. 'Put you in there, my lad, and we'll have two of you! Ha! Ha! Ha!' Mr Grottel said one day.

'How does it work? – the sawing in half trick?' Andrew looked at the box in question. Quick as a flash, Mr Grottel held up a saw from behind the counter.

'Want me to show you?'

'No thank you,' replied Andrew hastily. 'I'll just have those cards please.' And he had put down his money and left, thinking afterwards, how silly! – He's only trying to be funny! But somehow it didn't seem as funny as all that.

The morning that his father had brought him to Verbena Lodge, they had gone into the Magic Shop, as for some reason Mr Jamieson had thought that amongst all his other merchandise Mr Grottel might keep diaries.

'He won't, Dad, I'm positive,' Andrew said as he got out of the car.

'Just go in and ask, and if he doesn't, I'll pop into Terrys on the way home. I've lost mine, and I must get another before we go away.' Andrew's parents were going for a week to France.

The shop, as usual, was empty, and there was no sign of Mr Grottel. Andrew stood for a little while, once more completely captivated by the strange assortment of objects surrounding him. The usual collection of dummies; a great pile of amber beads heaped together in an open suitcase, and in front of him on the glass-topped counter, a mirror which he had not seen before. It was a puzzle, because however much he looked at it and from whatever angle, he could only see his own face reflected, not what was behind him. There were the usual piles of books, and what looked like old clothes; and beside the box where you could be sawn in half and maybe come out whole again, was another larger box, big enough for someone of his height to walk straight into. It was black, and had 'Vanishing Trick' painted on the side in red. Andrew walked over to it, and put his hand on the catch. He had always wanted to know how this particular trick worked; now was his chance to find out. He unfastened the catch and opened the door.

Whatever he had expected, it wasn't what he saw. Inside it was like a little room, walls, floor and ceiling lined with black silk; and hanging from a hook was a silver bird-cage. In the cage was a small bird, a beautiful golden colour, with an orange beak and a grey ring round its neck. Seeing the light, it began to flutter and scrabble at the bars of the cage, as if trying to find a way out. Poor thing, thought Andrew. What a horrid place to keep a bird. At that moment there was a movement from the doorway at the back of the shop, and he heard Mr Grottel's voice.

'Who's that? Is someone there?' Andrew was obscured by the box, and he just had time to shut the door again before Mr Grottel saw him.

'What are you doing young man, eh? Snooping around as usual? Hoping to discover some of my secrets, eh? eh?'

'Why do you keep that poor bird in there?' Andrew said. 'I shouldn't think there's much air for it.'

Mr Grottel leaned over the counter, and stared at Andrew over the tops of his spectacles.

'What bird?' he said.

'That one!' Andrew pointed at the box, 'in there!'

'Oh! – the Vanishing Trick!' Mr Grottel said, smiling his peculiar smile. 'Just keeping it for my partner. Did you know I had a partner now? Oh yes, we shall be rich. Rich beyond anything you had ever imagined! Rich beyond your wildest dreams!'

'Really?' murmured Andrew. Being rich was not one of the things he often thought about.

'Open the door again!'

Andrew unfastened the catch again, and peered inside.

'But – it's empty!' he stammered.

'Yes, it's a trick. Unusual, isn't it? But then my partner is – er – unusual.' He smiled again in a thoroughly disconcerting way, and rubbed his large flabby hands together. 'Anything else you're interested in – while you're here?'

'Yes – that mirror,' Andrew said, forgetting all about his father's diary. 'I can see my face in it, but – well – there's no reflection behind me, is there?'

'Perhaps it doesn't reflect the place where you think you are!'

'What?'

'You think you are, where you seem to be, don't you? But supposing you aren't – where you think you are? . . .' Mr Grottel began to laugh, a queer high-pitched cackling sound, and rocked himself gently backwards and forwards behind the counter.

Absolutely bonkers, thought Andrew. Aloud he said, 'Have you any diaries?' Mr Grottel shook his head slowly. 'I thought not. I'll tell Dad. Good morning.'

The bell tinkled as he opened the door; and as he sat down beside his father, he looked back through the car window. Mr Grottel was still standing behind the counter smiling faintly, watching them.

'He's batty,' Andrew said, as his father started the engine. 'Quite apart from being peculiar.'

'He was rather a famous magician at one time,' Mr Jamieson said. 'I suppose it went to his head.' They both laughed, and for the time being Andrew forgot about Mr Grottel.

A wind rustled the leaves above him; the air felt suddenly colder. Andrew sat up, and took the telescope out of his pocket. Well, at any rate, now he would be able to see the back of the shop better. He was about to raise it to his eye, when something below him caught his attention, and made him forget about Mr Grottel and his shop for the time being.

14

Stepping carefully along the wall beneath him, a strange figure was approaching – a tall man completely enveloped in grey furs, a little round embroidered hat perched on his head. Over his shoulder, he carried a small grey sack. As he came closer, Andrew could see a long pointed face, a straggling beard, which somehow reminded him of icicles, and curiously light amber-coloured eyes. It was an interesting face, but not a nice one. When he was almost exactly beneath the hidden platform, he sat down on the wall, putting the sack beside him; and all that could be seen was the top of the embroidered hat, and a bit of his grey furs.

Now Andrew was a boy like other boys; and the sight of that embroidered hat, for all the world like a target, directly beneath him, was too much. He picked up one of the many dead sticks which lay on his platform, and

taking careful aim, let it drop on the figure below. But it missed. He selected another thicker stick, and dropped that. It was a better shot, and only missed by a hair's breadth. The third stick was much thicker than the other two, more of a cudgel you might say, and he had had some practice. That one didn't miss. Andrew quickly withdrew his head so as not to be seen. He was prepared for something to happen; shouting, angry words, a row, but not for what actually did happen. When he poked his head over the edge of the platform again, the man had gone! Vanished! Not a trace of him! Well – that's not quite true. The sack that he had been carrying was lying at the foot of the wall, and as Andrew looked at it, he thought he saw it move.

He began to climb down the tree; always slower going down than climbing up. At last he was there. To his surprise the ground beneath the chestnut was speckled with white flakes. He touched the grass, and found it ice-cold. It's frost! he thought. How extraordinary! Frost in June! He looked around for a glimpse of the intruder, but saw nothing. From the sack, however, came the sound of scuffling. Andrew knelt down on the frosty grass, and taking his penknife from his pocket, cut the string round the neck of the sack, and opened it. Immediately there was a great flurry and flapping, and three pigeons flew out. Or were they doves? Andrew wasn't quite sure. They soared into the air, and wheeling sharply above him, were soon out of sight. He was about to pick up the sack when there was more fluttering, and another bird hopped out on to the grass. This one was smaller, and in no hurry to go. A golden yellow, with a ring of grey round its neck, it stepped nervously across the grass, as if uncertain which direction to take. Andrew held out his hand. The bird, after staring at him with bright suspicious eyes for a moment or two, took a few steps forward, and jumped on to his hand. He was almost certain that this was the bird he had seen in Mr Grottel's shop. At any rate, it looked exactly the same.

'Where was he taking you?' Andrew whispered, holding his hand very still. The bird opened its beak as if it might be going to answer his question, but only made a harsh croaking sound. Then, bowing its head several times, it suddenly opened its wings and flew up above his head, higher and higher, until it too was lost to view. Perhaps the poor thing was trying to say thank you, Andrew thought.

He was about to retrieve his bike, and go back to the house, when he saw something else lying in the long grass under the wall; something that glinted and shone in the sunlight. He bent down, and picked up a little hand mirror. It was not unlike the one he had seen in Mr Grottel's shop the other day, but smaller, with an elaborately wrought silver frame, and pale pinkish glass. Examining it more closely, he realised that actually it was rather odd. Because, if he stared into it, he could see his own face reflected; at the same time he could also look through at the gardens beyond. So it was both a mirror and a kind of eye-glass as well.

He stood for a moment turning this strange object over in his hand, thinking about the man he had seen walking along the wall. It must belong to him; who else? Finally he slipped the little thing into his pocket, and pushing his bike, walked slowly towards the house.

Tea was on the table, and his grandmother and Miss Shooter were sitting eating scones in front of the fire – summer and winter there was always a fire at Verbena Lodge.

'Hullo Darling!' screeched Scratchit from the top of the bookcase.

'Gran!' Andrew said, helping himself to a scone, 'who lives in that house you can only see the roof of?'

'Which house?' His grandmother poured out a third cup of tea.

'Marry me! Marry me!' croaked Scratchit.

'Don't interrupt,' Andrew said, 'or I'll put you in your cage. The one with no front door – you can only see the roof.'

'Oh the house that looks as if it isn't there?'

'I think so.'

'That's where Mr Grottel lives; his shop is on the other side. Why? – have you lost a ball in his garden?' Andrew shook his head. 'Mr Grottel *is* a bit peculiar, I think,' Mrs Jamieson said for no reason. 'But then so, of course, are many of us.'

But Andrew wasn't listening. As clear as if it had been with them in the room, an image of the Dragon Clock rose before his eyes; and in his imagination he found himself examining the painting on the lacquered case. 'I'll be back in a minute,' he said, and ran upstairs.

Facing him across the landing, the Dragon Clock struck the quarter hour, solemnly and slowly, as if it was the most important thing in the world. For a moment or two, Andrew stood studying it carefully. Something had changed; but he couldn't decide what it was. Then he saw – the picture! It was hard to believe, but the painted picture below the clock was different. Princess Plumpearl was no longer standing on the bridge, and in the corner, just showing above the strange flowerlike trees, were the turrets and battlements of another palace or castle. That one looks more like a fort, thought Andrew, taking a step forward. And there! – in the middle distance beneath the trees, was a figure that had not been there before, or was it that he just hadn't noticed? No, he was sure. Whoever it was standing there in the shadows staring straight back at him, had not been there the last time he looked at the picture.

18

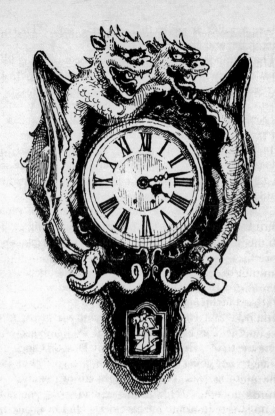

'Gran!' he said as he sat down in front of the fire, 'you haven't – er – changed that picture on the Dragon Clock in any way, have you?' He knew as he said it what the answer would be.

'No of course not, dear. Why should I?'

'It's – different now. Quite different.'

'Well, it always was rather indistinct, wasn't it? I can't really remember it.'

'I remember it perfectly,' Andrew said. 'There's a figure gone, and another one come!'

'That's impossible, dear! You must be imagining it!'

But Andrew knew that he wasn't imagining it. The figure on the bridge had gone; and another one was standing under the trees. And although he wasn't exactly frightened or alarmed, he felt uncomfortable, ill at ease, as if there was something that was not as it should be.

He was silent for a moment, and then, when Miss Shooter had gone to fetch some more hot water, he said, 'Do you think anyone would poach pigeons, or doves round here?' He described the man he had seen.

'Oh people will do anything,' Mrs Jamieson replied cheerfully. 'You do get the odd tramp sleeping in The Gardens in the summer; they might fancy a pigeon or two.'

'I don't think he was a tramp.' He had a queer feeling about that man. He shivered slightly. What was he doing with that sackful of birds?

'It's odd that you should ask about Mr Grottel,' his grandmother continued. 'I had a note from him last week, asking me to tea. He wants to buy my Dragon Clock.'

'You're not going to sell it to him, are you?' For some unaccountable reason he felt a slight stir of anxiety.

'Certainly not!' Mrs Jamieson replied tartly. 'Certainly not; but I should like to see his clocks. He has a collection too, you know. I'm going on Tuesday. You can come with me if you wish.'

Andrew didn't answer. He was thinking about those strange yellowy eyes, and the little bird in the sack. He was almost sure that it was the same as the one in the cage in Mr Grottel's shop.

2 Disappearance

Tuesday was wet and cold. The wind blew in fitful gusts, and roared down the chimney as if it intended to strip the roof off. The Gardens had a dripping sodden appearance. It was altogether more like March than July.

In the morning Andrew and his grandmother went shopping. He still had some money left from his birthday, and he wanted to spend it on a set of cogs and wheels for his Meccano set. When they got back to Verbena Lodge they were cold and their feet wet through. After lunch Andrew settled down in front of the fire, and started to build a complicated mechanical device which very cleverly included all the cogs and wheels he had bought that morning. His grandmother sat knitting and reading at the same time, a remarkable feat which never failed to astonish Andrew. The afternoon passed rapidly, and it seemed no time at all before the fifteen clocks on the mantelpiece were beginning to strike four.

'It's time for me to go round to Mr Grottel,' Mrs Jamieson said, closing her book. 'Do you want to come?'

'I think I'd rather stay here. It's so nice and warm,' Andrew replied screwing another wheel into place, and turning it so that four other wheels began to revolve slowly.

'I don't blame you,' his grandmother said. 'But don't bother Miss Shooter, will you? She's got a headache and

wants to lie down.' Andrew promised to leave Miss Shooter in peace. 'If I'm not back by six, you can send out a search party!' Mrs Jamieson laughed, and picked up her gloves from the table. 'I don't suppose I'll be as long as that,' she said and shut the door.

The rest of the afternoon went very quickly. Andrew fetched Scratchit downstairs to keep him company; but he was more of a nuisance than a help, because he kept trying to eat the nuts and screws, and fly off with bits of Meccano in his beak.

'Marry me! Marry me!' he screeched from the top of the bookcase with his beak full of screws.

'I'll strangle you if you don't give me my screws,' Andrew said.

At five o'clock Miss Shooter came downstairs, and said that her headache was still bad, but she was going to make a cup of tea, as she thought it would do her good. They had some tea and toast in front of the fire, and then just before six, Miss Shooter decided that although her head was better, she needed some fresh air, and a turn round the block would get rid of her headache altogether.

'You'll probably meet Gran,' Andrew said.

It was six o'clock. All over the house the clocks began to strike and chime. The three grandfather clocks in the hall boomed out their solemn notes; the cuckoo clocks clucked and clattered upstairs; chimes and bells, clicks and whirrs, could be heard in every part of the house; and above them all, like a gong or a church bell ringing over distant hills, sounded the Dragon Clock.

At ten past six he heard his grandmother's key in the front door lock. When she came into the room, she was carrying a large square parcel.

'Look what I've got!' she said, putting it down on the floor in front of Andrew.

'What is it? Another clock?'

'No – quite different, but very beautiful. It's a work-box. Have a look!' She undid the string, and took off the outer wrappings carefully. It was very beautiful. A large, black rectangular box, inlaid with glistening mother-of-pearl. When it was opened, it was quite deep, and fitted with a tray lined with blue velvet. The tray was full of little velvet-covered boxes, with mother-of-pearl handles, and an assortment of coloured silks, ribbons, pins, tangles of wool, and all the other things that are generally to be found in a work-box. Set into the inner side of the lid, which was also lined with velvet, was a mirror.

'Where did you get it?' Andrew asked.

'Mr Grottel has lent it to me,' Mrs Jamieson said. 'I think he's trying to persuade me to change my mind about the Dragon Clock. He's terribly keen to buy it. By

23

the way, did you know he's got a partner now? Another magician. Greyling, I think he said.'

'You won't sell the clock, will you?'

'Certainly not! Now I must show this to Miss Shooter!'

'Miss Shooter's out for a walk,' Andrew said. 'Didn't you meet her? She said she was going round the block. Perhaps she's back, and I didn't hear her come in.'

'I'll go and see.' Mrs Jamieson shut the work-box and put it on the table. 'Be careful, Andrew, as it's not mine.'

Andrew stood by the table and looked at the decorations on the top of the box. They were different from the diamond-shaped lozenges on the side; and he realised with a slight shock that the intricate swirling patterns on the top were actually not flowers as he had thought, but strange half-real beasts; tails curled in convoluted loops, necks outstretched, wings beating on air – or rather on the black shiny surface of the work-box.

Dragons! he thought, stroking the top of the box with his finger tips. More dragons! He opened the lid to look once more at the contents; and as he did so, happened to glance into the mirror. He stared, and then gasped. Just for a second the face that gazed back at him and smiled so mockingly, was not his own. Then quick as a flash it had gone; and there again was his own face, the face he knew so well.

Frowning with perplexity and amazement, he banged the lid shut and stood thinking. He knew that other face, he'd seen it before. That pointed chin, and long nose; the man with the sackful of birds under the chestnut tree. He was sure it was him. But it wasn't possible – was it? He must have just imagined the other face. But he knew he was deceiving himself. As sure as sure, a face not his own had stared back at him, just for an instant.

'No, she's not back!' Mrs Jamieson said as she came bustling in to the room. 'She must have gone further.'

'What? Oh yes, Miss Shooter . . .' Andrew spoke with an effort. 'Gran,' he said slowly, 'I don't think you ought to keep that box.'

'Why ever not?'

'I don't know quite. But I think you should take it back. Anyway, out of the house.'

'Out of the house? Why?'

'I think . . . I think there's something . . . well, wrong with it; bad about it. I think it may harm us!'

'Harm us? How can it? A work-box? Andrew! You've been reading too many stories. I'm going to lock it, and it's going up to my room out of harm's way.' Mrs Jamieson picked up the box.

'Perhaps it will be all right if it's locked,' Andrew said.

'I don't know what you mean, dear. Now, if you get the patience cards out, we'll have a game in a minute.'

Andrew followed his grandmother out into the hall, and

took down his jacket. The little mirror he had found in the garden, was it still there? Yes, he could feel it in the inside pocket. How small it was, and fragile. He held it up to the light. The face he had just seen, and the man walking along the garden wall, were one and the same person, he felt sure. Did this mirror belong to him too? He stood for a moment in the hall deep in thought, and started when Scratchit landed suddenly on his shoulder.

'Hullo Darling!' the parrot murmured in his ear.

'Go away, I'm busy!' Andrew said, but he laughed all the same; and returning to the table by the fire began to lay out the patience cards.

Seven o'clock came and went. Eight o'clock, eight-thirty, and still no sign of Miss Shooter. When the clocks began to strike nine, Andrew could see that his grandmother was beginning to get fidgety.

'What on earth can have happened to her?' she said finally. 'This is not like Miss Shooter. Terribly inconsiderate to go for such a long walk.'

'You don't think she's had an accident?' Andrew said suddenly.

'I sincerely hope not,' Mrs Jamieson replied rather crossly. 'It would be very inconvenient just now. What can she be doing? You go to bed, Andrew dear. How tiresome – I don't know if she took her key. I shall have to wait up for her.'

Andrew took himself off to bed, but once there he could not sleep. It was quite dark when he thought he heard voices below. He sat up in bed and listened. Must be Miss Shooter come back. He got out of bed, and went to look down into the hall. He shivered; it was cold on the landing, and no wonder. He looked through the banisters and saw the front door wide open, letting a cold draught of air rush up the stairs. Whatever's going on? he thought.

'Gran?' he called. No answer. It was absolutely still and quiet, a strange quietness that seemed all wrong in this house. Then he realised that all the clocks had stopped. He couldn't hear a single one ticking – except the one behind him, the Dragon Clock. He stood for a moment gazing up at the clock; it was five minutes to twelve. Then he turned, and opened the door to his grandmother's bedroom. The room was empty, the bed had not been slept in. But on the floor where she had left it was the work-box. The lid was open, and the contents were strewn all around it.

3   Princess Plumpearl

Cold and confused, Andrew stood shivering on the darkened landing wondering what to do.

Well! The first thing was to shut the front door. He ran down the stairs and crossed the hall, pausing for a moment to slip on his jacket which he saw hanging with all the other coats by the downstairs cloakroom. He was about to slam the front door shut, when something on the top step made him hesitate. A bird, head craning this way and that, was staring at him anxiously, as if not quite sure whether to stay or go. Andrew recognised the golden bird he had rescued from the sack a day or two before. He held out his hand.

'Come in!' he said. 'I think I need all the friends I can get.' The bird hopped in through the door, and Andrew shut it quickly. From the upstairs landing, a familiar voice called 'Hullo! Hullo!' and Scratchit's face could be seen peeping through the banisters.

'Oh Scratchit!' Andrew said, as he made his way upstairs, the golden bird following. 'I don't know what's going on!' With Scratchit perched on his shoulder he felt better. He switched the light on, and closed his grand-mother's door. As he did so, the Dragon Clock began to strike twelve. One . . . two . . . three . . . The deep solemn notes rang out in the silent house. There was a harsh

squawk from behind him, and Andrew turned, and drew in his breath sharply. The bird, with its shiny plumage, no longer looked the same. It had been a small and dainty creature, with its bright eyes and small orange feet. Now it was much bigger, and somehow taller – with its beak disappearing, the eyes getting larger, and its legs straightening and becoming longer. Andrew gasped. It hardly looked like a bird. In fact it wasn't any more. There was a face appearing, where a moment earlier the beak had protruded: the rosy young face of a girl about his own age, or a little younger. There were still a few feathers growing where the hair should have been. But mostly it was there, glossy black hair, fastened in heavy swathes about her head. Four . . . five . . . six . . . Fascinated, he could see a golden necklace forming round her neck. Her clothes appeared, a satin jacket, sprinkled with silver and pearls, dark richly coloured skirts, still with a few feathers clinging to them, and over everything, a gleaming golden cloak, which stuck out from her body in stiff, heavy folds. Seven . . . eight . . . nine . . . boomed the clock. Andrew stared unable to believe his eyes. Ten . . . eleven . . . twelve . . . midnight, and the transformation was complete. She stood before him, the bird girl, small and graceful, a slight smile lighting up her face.

He recognised her at once, of course, as he had always known he would.

'I think I know you,' he said, hesitating a little, it seemed so ridiculous, 'don't I?'

The girl nodded, smoothing down her skirts nervously.

'You are the Parrot Boy?' her voice was soft and gentle.

'What? Oh! – Scratchit you mean?' Andrew glanced at Scratchit on his shoulder. 'Yes, that's right.' He wasn't sure what she meant. 'Do you know my name?' The girl shook her head. 'I know yours!' He felt rather proud. 'It's – Plumpearl – isn't it?'

The girl smiled again, and took a step forward. 'You are in great danger,' she said, her hand on his arm, 'in great danger. You can come with me if you wish, but we must leave here at once, while there is still time.' She glanced behind her briefly, as if she expected to see someone standing in the corner of the landing.

For the first time, Andrew felt faintly alarmed. 'Go? I can't go anywhere! I'm supposed to be in bed; and anyway my grandmother . . .' he broke off uncertainly, turning towards his grandmother's empty room.

'Yes?' the girl said. 'Your grandmother . . .?'

'Well – I don't know where she is. She's gone – vanished. So has Miss Shooter,' he added.

'Where? Where have they gone?'

'I'm afraid I don't know,' Andrew said rather miserably, and he began to tell her of all the things that had happened during the afternoon and evening. His grandmother's visit, Miss Shooter's disappearance, the voices he had heard in the hall; and how he was just coming down to shut the front door, when he had seen the little bird on the front steps.

'But how did he get in?' the girl said as if to herself. 'Your grandmother, she didn't invite anyone this evening, did she? Have any visitors I mean?'

Suddenly Andrew remembered the work-box and he described the face he had seen for an instant in the mirror.

'It was the man – with – with – with the sack!' Andrew said, 'I think.' He was beginning to feel frightened in spite of himself.

'Quick then. We mustn't waste any more time.'

She turned, and standing very straight before the Dragon Clock, began to speak rapidly in a low voice, words that sounded strange and foreign, and that he could not understand. Now she was waving her arms and chanting; he still could not make out the words. She was getting

31

more and more excited; her voice rising almost to a scream. Scratchit fidgeted on his shoulder muttering and croaking.

'What are you going to . . . ?' he broke off his sentence halfway. The Clock! What was happening to the Clock? It, too, was changing.

'They're coming – they're coming now,' the girl said.

'Who are coming?' Andrew asked, staring at the Clock.

The red lacquer shone under the hard glare of the landing light. He took a step back. Was he imagining it, or were the dragons getting larger?

'Look!' the girl whispered. 'They're beginning to move – do you see?' It was true. Slowly, as if with an immense effort, the two dragons lifted their heavy heads, and swung them outwards in the air above him. They were getting larger – their tails writhing and thrashing on the sides of the clock – larger and more lifelike every moment. They were too big for the clock; they would topple off it. . . . Yes! With a dry rustling sound which made Andrew shudder, first one then the other, slid down the wall, and stood before them, squat and scaly, swinging their great heads from side to side, and opening and shutting their ferocious jaws.

On the wall behind them, the clock kept up its slow rhythm, like water dripping in some vast forgotten cave.

Andrew stood as one in a trance, staring at the huge beasts that crouched before him.

'This is not a good place to be at the moment!' From a long way off, he heard the girl's voice, 'Come with us – we'll help you if we can.'

'Who is we?' Andrew asked, still gazing at the dragons.

'All of us! My father, everyone at the Palace. You have no idea where your grandmother has gone?'

'Well – I suppose she might just have gone for a walk,' Andrew replied, knowing as he said it that this certainly wasn't what had happened.

The girl went to the window, and stood with her face pressed to the glass, looking out into the night beyond. Scratchit muttered and murmured in his ear, and Andrew shivered. Anything would be preferable to staying in this deserted, unrecognisable house.

'All right!' he said, 'I'll come. But I must get my shoes, and some jeans.' This didn't take long, and soon he was back. 'I'm ready! Where do we go?'

Princess Plumpearl unfastened the window catch, and beckoned to him.

'It's no use trying to take the clock,' she said as if to herself. 'Anyway he won't be able to use it with the dragons gone.'

'What? Who?'

'Come! You go first – we must make haste. Ride on him,' she added pointing at the nearest dragon. 'I'll follow. He will know what to do.'

'But – where are we actually going?' stammered Andrew, gazing horrified first at the dragon and then at the open window.

'We will try and get across the forest to the First Lodge. We'll be safe there for one night.'

'What forest? There's no forest near here – unless you mean the park? What forest do you mean?'

The girl looked at him for a moment, opened her mouth to speak, and then stopped as a heavy knocking started on the door downstairs. Scratchit's claws tightened on his shoulder.

'Quick!' whispered Plumpearl, 'I'll follow.' The knocking sounded again, and Andrew thought he could hear voices as well.

The two dragons waited by the open window, sniffing at the night air, their wings half open, their long barbed tails thrashing gently from side to side. Hesitating no longer, he jumped astride the beast nearest him. He felt the muscles of the shoulders tense beneath him, and in one swift movement it was on the sill.

'Hold on Scratchit!' he said, gripping the spiny mane with both hands and pressing his legs into the animal's sides. With a sickening lurch, the dragon sprang; he felt the first downward strokes of the wings, and then they were rushing headlong through the night air.

4 Flight

Although it was after midnight, the sky was still quite light;
a pale greeny blue, with a few stars showing over to the
west. Looking down, Andrew expected to see the lights of
London spread out beneath him, but there was nothing; it
was completely dark and silent. No lights, and no sounds;
just black emptiness, a cold rush of air past his face, and the
noise of great wings beating on either side of him.

'Why do you think there are no lights down there?' he
called, when he saw that Plumpearl and her dragon had
drawn level with them.

'There's nothing but the forest beneath us! – until we
get to the Lodge. Just trees!' He heard her voice faintly
against the wind, then she overtook him, and he was flying
directly behind her.

Andrew stared at the black void beneath him. As far as
he could judge they should just about be over the Bayswater Road. Perhaps she meant Hyde Park? And yet it
seemed odd that there were no lights at all. He twisted his
head and stared anxiously in the direction from which
they had come. He could see nothing, and nothing ahead
either.

'How far . . . is . . . where did you say we were going?' he
shouted.

'The First Lodge . . . lights . . . down there . . . we should
see lights . . . !' Her voice was lost again on the wind.

He felt very unsafe. The dragon he was clinging to was quite a large animal, its hard horny skin smooth and slippery. His fingers were getting numb, and it was difficult to get a good grip with his legs. He put his arms round the dry scaly neck, and held on as best he could.

'There it is!' shouted the Princess, pointing. 'Down there!' Straining his eyes, he followed her gesture, and at last made out far below them, some pinpoints of light, twinkling like stars. 'The Lodge!' called Plumpearl. '. . . nearer than I thought.'

Without warning, the two dragons spread out their huge wings on either side like sails, and began to plunge downwards. The wind whistled past, tugging at his hair and clothes, almost tearing him from his perch. Andrew put up a hand to hold on to Scratchit, and was horrified to find him no longer there.

'I've lost Scratchit!' he called frantically; but he knew she couldn't hear him, and breathless and giddy, he put his head down on the dragon's bony shoulders, and prayed that Scratchit would find his own way down.

They landed in a small flat courtyard, somewhere in a huddle of dimly lit low buildings. Almost before their feet touched the ground, Plumpearl was hurrying across the cobbles, her skirts flying out behind her. Now she was knocking on a wooden door at the side of the yard. Andrew dismounted slowly, rubbed his cold knees, and stood gazing up at the sky, black now because of the lights. He felt lost and miserable without Scratchit. Was he up there somewhere? he wondered. More important, would he find his way down?

Plumpearl tapped once more on the door. 'I don't think anyone is here,' she said. Her voice was frightened. 'I don't know what to do if . . . if . . .'

'Perhaps you aren't knocking loudly enough,' Andrew interrupted. 'Here, let me have a go,' and he banged on the door with all his force, and then again with both hands. 'Who is it you want anyway?'

'The Green Man and the Foresters live here,' Plumpearl whispered. 'I think they'll help us if they can.' Andrew knocked again, and after what seemed a long time, they heard footsteps approaching. A small barred slot in the door opened, and a pair of eyes stared at them suspiciously.

'Who is knocking at the Lodge at this hour of the night?' a rather cross voice said from within.

'We have come to see the Green Man. Please let us in!' Plumpearl said at once.

'He is sleeping!'

'Please let us in – we need help!'

'A lot of people come to us for help – who are you?'

'I am Princess Plumpearl, daughter of the Emperor of Kon.'

'Who? Speak up, please.'

37

'Princess Plumpearl – and a – er – companion. Here is my chain and seal, so you can be sure.' Plumpearl took the heavy golden chain from round her neck, and passed it through the grille. 'We are unarmed,' she added.

There was a pause. Then the voice said, 'Unarmed? Wait a minute, please.' The eyes disappeared, and another pair took their place. There followed a lengthy discussion which they could only hear snatches of, as to whether they should be admitted or not. Plumpearl looked up at the sky nervously.

'I wish they'd hurry,' she said. 'We are not safe until we are inside this building.' But at last, after her necklace had been returned to her through the grille, the door was finally opened; and with relief they slipped inside, to find several small elderly men dressed in foresters' suits and armed with clubs and knives, standing clustered together regarding them anxiously.

However, once they had seen that there was nothing terribly dangerous about Plumpearl or her companion, they became more friendly, and without more ado, led them upstairs.

The Green Man was not asleep, but sat reading, propped up on pillows, in a large four-poster bed. Even sitting down, he was a tall majestic figure, with a long greenish-grey beard. His face, too, had a greenish tinge; but it could have been reflected light from the pillows and sheets, which were also green.

The Green Man closed his book, bade them sit beside him, and shook his head gravely as he listened to their story.

'These are evil, evil days,' he sighed at last.

'I could not have escaped on my own,' Plumpearl said, looking at Andrew.

'Well – I haven't done anything really . . .'

'You must get to Kon,' the Green Man interrupted. 'You will be safe there; and they will know where to look for your grandmother.'

'I've lost my parrot too,' murmured Andrew. The truth was he felt almost more worried about Scratchit than Mrs Jamieson. She was pretty good at looking after herself, but he wasn't so sure about Scratchit. He was such an idiot!

'We shall be honoured to have you as our guests, Ma'am; and you must, of course, do as you wish. But the forest is a dangerous place nowadays.' He shrugged his shoulders. 'Even my domain is not as safe as it used to be.' He gazed at Andrew with admiring eyes. 'You are a brave lad. There are not many who would dare to do as you have done!'

What have I done exactly, Andrew thought to himself, but he was too tired to say anything. The big room was very warm, and he found it harder and harder to pay attention to the other two. He was almost asleep, his head nodding forward on to his chest, when he realised he was being spoken to, and opened his eyes with an effort.

'Do you live in the forest? I don't remember seeing you before,' the Green Man said kindly.

'I'm – er – staying with my grandmother at present,' Andrew replied, 'at Verbena Lodge. But . . .'

'She's the one that has disappeared?' Andrew nodded his head wearily. This is a dream he thought, shutting his eyes again. In a minute I'm going to wake up, and then they'll all be gone. It's just a silly dream, and soon I'll wake up in my own bed. He opened his eyes, to find the Green Man leaning forward smiling at him.

'Poor lad, you're dropping with sleep! We must rest now, and in the morning I will put you on the right road.'

He pulled aside the coverlet, and got out of bed. Then, halfway across the room, he stopped suddenly, and turned towards them, putting his finger to his lips.

Outside the window, they all heard a faint scratching and scuffling, like the branch of a tree scraping against a pane of glass.

'Do not be alarmed, nobody can get in here,' their host whispered. 'All the windows are barred.'

Slowly he walked towards the window, and drew aside one curtain. After a moment, he smiled, unfastened the catch, and to Andrew's delight Scratchit appeared through the bars. He sidled along the curtain rail, looking down at them sideways.

'Hullo Darling!' he croaked, in his raucous voice, and flew down to perch on Andrew's shoulder.

Andrew sighed. He knew then he wasn't going to wake up, because it wasn't a dream.

In the morning one of the Foresters roused them with bowls of warm milk, flavoured with honey, and some little scones still hot from the oven.

They were lying on the floor of the room where the Green Man had left them the night before, wrapped in furs and rugs. On either side of them the two dragons kept watch, their bulging eyes turned alternately to the window and the door.

Andrew stretched himself, and pulled the rug up under his chin. Usually he detested warm milk, but today he was so hungry that he gulped it down, and ate all the scones he was given, only keeping a few crumbs back for Scratchit. When the Forester had left the room he said, 'I want to know exactly where we are going! I mean – well – I don't think I should start off on a long journey just anywhere. I'd rather go back to Verbena Lodge.'

'What about your grandmother?'

'Well . . .'

'I don't think you'll find your grandmother there! And anyway it wouldn't be safe to go back at present.'

Plumpearl hesitated. 'Tell me, does she have the key to the Dragon Clock?'

'Yes,' replied Andrew. 'Well – she did. Actually I've got it at the moment. She asked me to take it upstairs, and I forgot. Usually she keeps it on her dressing table.'

The Princess put down her bowl of milk. 'That explains it,' she said.

'What explains what?'

'Why she's disappeared.'

'Does it? Not to me!'

'She is the Keeper of the Clock!'

'The what? I don't know what you are talking about!' interrupted Andrew almost angrily. 'It's only a clock – I mean it's just an ordinary clock, isn't it?'

The Princess was silent, and before his eyes came a picture of the Dragon Clock as it had been the previous night: the gilded face, the lacquered ornamental case, and the scaly brick-red dragons sliding down the wall to crouch at his feet. Not a very ordinary clock when you thought about it.

'What do you mean, the Keeper of the Clock?' he said at last.

Plumpearl sighed. 'It's a long story, but I can tell you a little of it.' She went to the window and stood looking out. 'Many years ago, before I was born, or my mother and father, a great king, who was also a magician, lived at Kon: it was he who built the Palace there. And because he was a magician, he filled it with all manner of marvellously strange possessions, some of which had magical powers.'

'Clocks for instance?' Andrew said.

'Yes, many clocks. It is said that with some, he could even turn back time, and make it run again. Most powerful of all his possessions was the Dragon Clock. Eventually he died; and in the years that followed, many of the magical possessions vanished, or were broken or lost, until in my grandfather's day, there were only ten left. And it is on these possessions that the power of Kon rests.'

'What are they?'

'The Dragon Clock, its key — for without the key eventually it will run down. The Keeper of the Clock. The two red dragons, who are Guardians of the Clock. A picture. The golden chain and seal,' she touched the necklace round her neck. 'The great emerald and ruby throne in the Palace of Kon; and the Golden Sword which hangs above it, and whose owner and only he, will the Dragon Peoples obey. These are the only possessions that we have left; and without which we are powerless. Whoever has these — and me — is the Ruler of Kon.

Plumpearl turned to face him. 'He is collecting them one by one. He has the Picture and the Sword. He had the

Clock, but by some chance he lost it, or it was taken from him. He must have your . . .' Andrew interrupted her.

'Who? Who is collecting them? You haven't told me who?'

'The Greyling, the Enchanter from the frozen country at the northern edges of the forest. Some people call him the Ice Sorcerer, others the Grey Magician.'

'Greyling?' echoed Andrew, 'Greyling?' and he thought how strange it was, that he had never come across that name before, and now he had heard it twice in as many days.

The Princess continued. 'Since his coming, great parts of the forest are enchanted. The Dragon Peoples fight amongst themselves, and plot the downfall of Kon behind our backs, and everyone is afraid.'

It was odd that he should hear that name again. It must be a coincidence, of course, but Greyling was the name of Mr Grottel's new partner. Queer, too, that he should have seen the imprisoned bird for the first time in Mr Grottel's shop – if it was the same bird that is.

'What does he look like, this wizard fellow?' Andrew asked suddenly.

'He is tall, with a long white face; always dressed in furs to withstand the cold of his country. There is nothing particular about him, and yet he is terrible to look at. He . . .'

'Has he got – sort of – yellow eyes?' interrupted Andrew.

'Yes, like a cat's.' Plumpearl shivered. 'He is the cleverest magician we have ever known. And he is cruel. People say that where his heart should be there is only a lump of ice.'

'Sounds great!' Andrew said, holding out some crumbs for Scratchit.

Pulling the coverings aside, he got up, and went to the window. It was daybreak; everything bathed in the cold grey light of morning. Early as it was, however, the view from the window was magnificent. Beneath them, and on all sides, lay a great, dark forest. He had never before seen such a huge amount of land completely covered by trees.

'What is the name of this forest?' he said to the Princess.

'It is too big to have just one name, and nobody knows how far it stretches. It is "The Forest". Once long ago, it was all one kingdom, and safe for everyone. But now, everything is changed; and although parts of it are still inhabited, none of it is safe.'

'— And you think the Grey Thingummy or whatever he's called, has spirited away my grandmother and poor old Miss Shooter?'

Plumpearl nodded, and Andrew was about to ask some more questions, when there was a knock at the door, and the Green Man entered.

'Are you ready to leave?' he said, having first enquired

how they had slept. 'It would be better to start as early as we can. I shall accompany you, and put you on the right road. Take these cloaks, it can be cold in the forest, and anyway,' he looked at Plumpearl, 'it would be wiser to cover those clothes, Ma'am. One never knows who one might meet. Have you weapons?' Andrew shook his head, and the Green Man held out a stout stave, and two daggers as well. 'I have a basket of provisions for you – it is a long journey. Is there anything else we should do before you go?'

'We must get a message to my father,' Plumpearl said. 'I shall send one of the Guardians of the Clock.'

'But you should have them both with you! It would be unwise to walk through the forest unprotected!'

'We will take one, and send the other,' Plumpearl said calmly. 'Then my father's soldiers will come some of the way to meet us. Have you a pen and paper?'

She's not quite so gentle as she looks, thought Andrew; for a moment Plumpearl had reminded him of his grandmother – used to getting her own way. He wished heartily that he was setting off for Verbena Lodge. But there seemed no choice. Where could he go if he did not accompany her?

5   *The Forest*

The Green Man led the way, mounted on a small dun pony. Princess Plumpearl perched on the saddle before him, and Andrew, with Scratchit on his shoulder, and the dragon following, strode behind them whistling.

The forest was full of sunlight, and the sound of birds singing. Unfamiliar and strangely shaped flowers grew in the long grass beside the mossy track, and beneath the trees, rabbits ran and played. Once, Andrew thought he saw a fox. The trees themselves were very different from any that he had seen before. Tall and slender, they had large irregular leaves, or often only one or two leaves, and many brilliantly coloured flowers and fruits.

After a couple of hours, they halted. The trees had cleared briefly, and in front of them, a grassy stretch of ground sloped downwards. Across this, the path zig-zagged towards a small stream, bordered by rushes and clumps of forget-me-nots. A plank bridge straddled the stream, and on the further side the forest continued. But even from where they stood, Andrew could see a change: the trees darker, growing closer together, some-how forbidding. Not the sort of place one would choose to walk.

'My domain ends here,' the Green Man said. 'This is as far as I can take you. But as long as you keep to the pack road, you should be safe. Follow it as far as it goes, and you will see an ancient stone fountain. Take the right hand path, and by the end of the day, you will come to the Second Lodge. From there it is but a day's journey to the Palace of Kon. But this road takes you through the country of the Dragon Peoples, and you must be careful. As you know, they are perpetually at war with one another, and there are many dangers for the traveller. It would be better if you were accompanied on this part of your journey.'

'There may be some of my father's soldiers at the Second Lodge,' Plumpearl murmured. 'If they can get through.'

'I hope so.' Their guide frowned, and glanced towards the dark trees on the far side of the stream. 'Yes, it would be better if you had soldiers with you.'

'It sounds an awfully long trek,' Andrew remarked discouraged. 'Wouldn't it be easier to fly?' The Green Man shook his head.

'Easier, but very dangerous. Above the forest you would be seen at once; and anyway it is too far for one animal to carry you both. No, walking is best, even though the way is long.' He put his hands on their shoulders. 'Do not be tempted into any forest dwellings. Many parts of the forest are enchanted, and you do not know who will be in them.' He hesitated for a moment, fumbling in his pocket, then held out his hand. 'Take this!' he said, 'my Magic Ring! As long as you wear it, I shall be able to see you; and if I can, I will help you.'

The ring, made of a dull greenish substance, was set with a stone that looked so much like an eye, that Andrew found himself gazing at it as if bewitched, unable to put it on. In the end, he slipped it on to his thumb, as it was too big for his other fingers. The Green Man smiled at them. 'May Providence be with you, and keep you from harm,' he said, giving Plumpearl the basket. 'I will do what I can to aid you.'

They thanked him, said goodbye, and walked down the slope towards the stream, wondering what awaited them in the forest ahead.

At first the path was much as it had been. But gradually it began to change. The broad grassy track narrowed, and they were forced to walk one behind the other. No birds sang now; and the trees grew so close together, that they shut out the light, giving everything a pale sub-terranean look. With her heavy skirts and delicate satin slippers, Plumpearl soon tired of walking, and rode instead on the dragon, who, in spite of its ferocious appearance, seemed a docile animal and trundled along sedately, making very little noise for a beast of such enormous size.

After they had been travelling for several hours, they reached a small clearing, and decided to rest and have something to eat. The basket had been neatly packed, and inside, wrapped in leaves, were fruit, bread, and some white cheese, as well as a flask of clear, fresh-tasting water.

'This ring gives me the creeps,' Andrew said, twisting it round on his thumb. 'The stone is exactly like an eye – and it's – Oh! –' The Princess looked up. 'It blinked! I'm sure!'

'Yes, it is an eye, so wherever we are the Green Man can see us.'

Andrew glanced sideways at the ring and made a face. The eye, small and greenish brown, gazed up at him steadily.

After they had finished their meal, they lay half asleep in the long grass, while Scratchit walked round the basket searching for any crumbs they might have dropped.

'Why did you call me the Parrot Boy?' Andrew asked a little later. 'Was it just because of silly old Scratchit?'

'Before the Greyling stole it away, there was a picture hanging in the Painted Hall in the Palace of Kon,' replied Plumpearl drowsily. 'It had been there since before anyone can remember. It is of a boy, with a parrot on his shoulder. The legend is that one day he will save the people of Kon from destruction. It is one of the Possessions.' She smiled at him. 'I recognised you at once!'

'But how did you know it was me?' Andrew asked

mystified. 'I mean, no one's done any paintings of me – at least I don't think they have. Surely I would know?'

There was a pause for a moment, then Plumpearl said, 'How did you know my name?'

'Er – well – I just sort of knew it!'

'That's right,' she replied softly. 'I just *know* the painting is of you!'

Andrew tried another question. 'The man in The Gardens, who had you in the sack – is he . . . the . . . ?'

'Yes – that's the Greyling. He must have become careless to let you see him.'

'If he was there, he could be seen I suppose.' Andrew wound a piece of grass on to his finger, and then took it off again. *If he was there!* For no reason at all, he thought suddenly of the mirror on Mr Grottel's counter, and those curious words, 'Maybe you aren't where you think you are!' Where was he now he wondered? And where on earth was he going? One thing he was sure about; the man with the sackful of birds, and the face he had seen for that fleeting instant in the work-box mirror, were one and the same person. There was no doubt of that.

For a while they were both silent. 'What did he want you in that sack for anyway?' he said at last.

'I am heir to the throne. He must have me too.'

'Of Kon?'

'Yes,' Plumpearl waved her hand vaguely round her. 'One day I will rule over all this.'

'All of it? Is it one country then?'

'It should be; once it was – until the Greyling came. Since then everything has changed. The ice creeps across the plain from the northern edges of the forest; the Dragon Peoples have been set against each other, and lay their countries waste, and no one is safe.'

'But why does he want you particularly?' Andrew persisted.

'He will make me his wife. Then he can claim it all; the Kingdom of Kon, the country of the Dragon Peoples, the gold, and everything else besides.'

'I suppose you don't fancy that?' Andrew said, knowing very well what the answer would be.

'I would rather die a thousand times!' Plumpearl replied fiercely.

Andrew lay in the grass, looking up at the sky, thinking what a far-fetched story it all was. Still, if this was her explanation, he'd have to believe it. After all he hadn't a better one.

'I threw sticks at him, I think,' he said smiling. 'Your Grey Wizard or whatever he calls himself. He disappeared pretty quickly then . . . Oh!' Andrew sat up abruptly.

'What is it?' Plumpearl sat up too.

'I've just remembered something. He left this behind in the grass, at least I suppose it was him.' He took the little mirror from his pocket, and held it up. This time his face was not reflected, but he could see some of the trees and bushes before them. Suddenly, with a startled exclamation, he stared in to it more closely.

'That's funny!'

'What's the matter?'

'Well, I can see something else! I mean, it's all quite different. Buses, and a road, and that looks like – well, it looks like, how extraordinary – Bromley High Street!'

'Let me see!' She took the mirror from him, and sat silently for several minutes gazing into it. 'I can't see anything except my face and the trees,' she said finally. 'Are you sure?'

'Quite sure. Here – give it to me!' He held it up in front of him again. 'Yes – that's Bromley High Street. I often go there with Gran, when she visits Uncle David! He lives just up that road on the right . . .' His voice trailed away as he sat entranced watching the scene he knew so well. At first it was very faint, like looking at a familiar background through a colour transparency. Then, little by little, the background faded, the transparency grew stronger and more opaque, until the whole thing was in reverse. Bromley High Street was real, and he was looking at it through a pale transparent layer of tall trees and bushes. The new landscape, he noticed, had by now extended beyond the edges of the mirror, and the din of traffic was quite clear.

He turned to the Princess, and was alarmed to find that he could hardly see her. She was so very faint that in a moment she would vanish altogether.

With difficulty, Andrew shut his eyes, and kept them shut, at the same time throwing the mirror into the grass. When he opened them, the road and the buses had disappeared, and there was nothing but the silent forest round them.

'Did I – was I – beginning to vanish?' he asked slowly. The Princess nodded, her eyes wide and frightened. He glanced around at the trees and bushes.

'Look!' he said, smiling at her, 'don't worry, but I'm going to try it again. I promise I won't vanish altogether. I just want to see if the same place comes back.'

He picked up the mirror, held it in front of him, and gazed into it. Exactly the same thing happened; and in a very few moments Bromley High Street began to appear again – faint and shadowy at first, but becoming clearer every moment; and when he turned to look at Plumpearl, he could hardly see her.

Andrew laid the glass aside, and rubbed his eyes vigorously.

'Is it – the mirror?' asked Plumpearl, her voice trembling a little.

'I think so. It must be. I think it's a kind of, well . . .' he had been going to say key, but it didn't sound right; although keys do sometimes open things, thought Andrew. For some peculiar reason, he had stumbled into another world which seemed to exist in the same place as his own, but which was quite separate. How could he explain, when he didn't understand it himself?

'I think your world, and my world – are – well, different, apart; though it looks as if somehow they exist in the same place. Like two thoughts in one person's head, but going on at the same time. And this,' Andrew held up the little mirror, 'is the way through from you to me – like a sort of key. The thing is, once I've got back to – to – where I usually am, can I find my way here again? – To where you are, I mean?'

Plumpearl shook her head doubtfully. 'I don't know. He can – the Greyling – and last time he took me with him.' She shivered. 'But I don't know about you!'

Andrew picked up the mirror, and slipped it into his pocket. 'I think I'll hang on to it,' he said. 'You never know, it might come in useful – if ever I'm to get back, I mean.'

He got to his feet humming under his breath. For some reason, the sight of those buses roaring along beside the shops in the High Street had cheered him up. As long as it's all still there, he thought, and I can get at it. He pulled his cloak about him, Scratchit fluttered up on to his shoulder, and they started off once more.

They must have been walking for about half an hour, when they came to the stone fountain that the Green Man had spoken of. It was built in the centre of the path, marking the spot where the two tracks met and intersected. The dragon was thirsty and drank long and greedily from the trough into which the water flowed.

'I'm going to bathe my feet,' Andrew said. 'I think I've got a blister coming.'

But he had hardly taken off his shoes, when the Princess held up her hand. 'Listen!' she whispered. 'I can hear something . . . what is it? Horses' feet? Let's hide! . . . we don't know who . . .' but before she had finished speaking, there came into view, moving slowly along the track on their left, a long line of pack animals, so heavily laden with bales and boxes, that every now and then one of them staggered, as if unable to walk another step. Beside them, their backs bent, and their faces turned towards the ground, plodded a number of small figures. As they came nearer, Andrew could see that they carried picks and shovels, and their clothes were dusty and blackened as if they had been working underground.

'Oh! – it's the miners!' Plumpearl said relieved. 'That's lucky. Perhaps we can travel with them!'

'Who are they?'

'The miners – on their way through the forest with their gold.' She stepped forward on to the path, and hailed the man leading the column. He looked up sharply, gave a signal, and the whole long line came to an abrupt halt.

Maggins, the leader of the miners, was a small bent man, not much taller than Andrew, with long powerful arms, and extremely large feet. His eyes appeared very white and blue in his lined and blackened face; and his mouth, when he spoke, startlingly red. His clothes had once been coloured, but now they were quite black. He had an old woollen cap on his head, and a wide leather belt, decorated with gold and silver studs, was fastened round his waist. He greeted the children in a friendly way, and the other miners stood in a bunch behind him, staring at them with round dull-witted eyes. They all, Andrew noticed, had extremely sharp-looking knives tucked into their belts.

'You shouldn't be out in the forest on your own,'

Maggins said at last, after several minutes conversation. 'Where are you heading for?'

'The Second Lodge,' Plumpearl replied, 'we hope to . . .'

'It's no good going there,' Maggins interrupted. 'It's been burned down – flat. No one there at all as far as I know.'

'What about – the people – there?' Plumpearl asked quickly.

'Some got out, some didn't. I haven't heard what happened to them as got away. Fled to Kon I daresay.'

Plumpearl turned to Andrew with a frightened face. 'What shall we do now? It's no use going there!'

'Best travel with us,' Maggins suggested. 'If you are going to Kon – that's where we're going! It's getting towards the Dragon People now, and the forest is full of – them and worse!' He pointed to the dragon who was standing beside the Princess. 'But you'll be all right with

55

us!' He smiled at them kindly, and picked up his tools. 'I wouldn't like to think of you alone in this place. It's not safe for grown men, let alone children. But we must be on our way now as we have to reach the Middle Clearing by nightfall, and that will take us the rest of the afternoon pretty well. Walk with me in the front here, there is more room.'

The children agreed, and Andrew pulled on his shoes. The miners hoisted their sacks on to their shoulders, and the long procession began to move slowly through the forest once more.

At length, when his legs were aching, and he was thirsty, hungry, and heartily sick of the whole thing, they came to a large clearing, where all the trees had been felled. It was obvious that Maggins and his miners had been here many times before; and they set about making their camp without fuss, or any sign of fatigue. After the donkeys had been tethered, each man took a bundle of palings under his arm, and began knocking them in all round the edge of the clearing, sharpening the ends of each post, so that soon a formidable palisade surrounded them. A rough ring existed already, but it had many gaps in it.

No animal, dragon or otherwise, could get through that easily, thought Andrew with satisfaction, watching as the last stake was hammered home. Next the donkeys were turned loose to graze; and while some of the men busied themselves with the baggage and provisions, two of the miners began to build a fire.

There's enough wood there for a Guy Fawkes bonfire for the whole of London, thought Andrew. He turned to Maggins who was standing beside him.

'Who leaves all that wood ready for you?' he asked.

'Why we do, of course!' laughed the other. 'These clearings are each a day's journey from the other. We leave everything ready for the next party of miners, and they do the same for us. That's the only way we can get through. It's all right for them,' he pointed at Princess Plumpearl, who with her dragon beside her, was strolling through the long grass picking flowers, 'the quality, who don't have to do anything. But we're not like that. We're earth people; have to work, and work hard. Still, that's how it is —' he broke off. One of the miners had lit the fire, and now the flames shot upwards, sending out a shower of sparks.

'Oh! – they never learn! Damp it down! Damp it down!' shouted Maggins, running towards them. 'Mercy on us, you'll have the whole place alight if you don't look sharp.'

'What does he mean – earth people?' Andrew said, as Plumpearl came to sit beside him.

'They live under the earth, and mine the gold, and anything else they find. Then they bring it through the forest to us.'

'What do you do with it?' Andrew asked curiously.

'We build with it, and make it into things.'

'Build with gold?' repeated Andrew, astonished.

'Yes, of course! The whole Palace of Kon, and everything there is made of gold. That's why Greyling schemes against us. He wants the gold.'

Everything made of gold! To Andrew this seemed just as extraordinary as everything else. But to the Princess there was obviously nothing unusual about it.

'They've always brought us the gold – the Magic Gold of Kon! Anyway, they must! What else could they do with it? They don't know how to make all the beautiful things we fashion from it.'

'Do you pay them?' But Plumpearl didn't seem to understand the question. 'Do you give them anything in return?'

'We make their tools and weapons, and they take back

food for the whole year with them,' Plumpearl replied gently. 'They are quite satisfied.'

To Andrew, this seemed rather an odd arrangement. But he said no more. It was getting dark. He could see a few stars flashing high above them, and a cold wind stirred the tops of the trees.

'You brought any food with you?' Maggins called suddenly from the other side of the clearing. 'What about that bird you got there? We'll cook 'im in with our bit of meat if you like!'

Andrew got up hurriedly. 'It's very kind of you,' he said, 'but he's not really meant for cooking; and anyway we've got a few bits of bread left.'

'Well! that's no good, you better have some of ours.' Maggins pointed to a space in the ring of men now squatting round the fire. 'Sit yourself down there, and your young lady. Nobody never goes short in my company.'

There was a big pot slung over the fire, and the miners were roasting lumps of meat on the end of long skewers. The children watched, as one of them rose to his feet, and

walking round the circle of men, gave each one a flat hard cake or biscuit. Andrew nibbled his, and was surprised by its fresh nutty flavour. After a while, the pot was set before Maggins; and taking it in turns, each man dipped his cake into it. This together with a few blackened lumps of meat, was their meal. Andrew ate everything he was given, and thought he'd never tasted better food.

'Aye! Aye! A full belly is a comfortable thing!' Maggins wiped his mouth with the back of his hand, and began cleaning his knife in the grass. 'What about some music? Can you sing, boy.'

'I'm afraid not. I . . .'

'I'll make some music for you,' Plumpearl said; and she took from her pocket a tiny golden box, which, when she opened the lid, gave forth a gentle melancholy piping. The delicate notes rang out in the silent forest, and from what seemed a great distance away, came a faint echo. One by one, the miners wrapped their cloaks around them, and lay down where they were. Only Maggins sat, smoking his pipe, and staring out into the dark beyond the fire. At last Andrew pulled his furry cloak about him, and settled himself on the hard earth. Soon he, too, was asleep.

6   Dragon Country

They made an early start the next morning; and travelling slowly through the forest, reached a wide swiftly-flowing river at about three o'clock in the afternoon. Here, amidst huge boulders and fallen logs, the miners busied themselves with their camp; and Andrew and Plumpearl, accompanied by the faithful dragon, walked off along the river bank.

After a little way, Andrew, footsore after his long march, sat down on a flat rock, and put his feet in the water. Beside him, the dragon drank noisily.

'Over there,' Plumpearl pointed towards the opposite bank, 'the country of the two Dragon Kings begins.'

'You mean the ones that are always at war?'

'It's divided in half, between the Black and the Red Dragon Kings. They used to live peacefully together, and the Red Dragon People were our friends. But now they are always fighting; they hate each other. Beyond them, a day's journey from here, is the Palace of Kon.' She sighed. 'I wish we could cross tonight.'

'Oh I think it's rather nice here,' Andrew said, wriggling his toes in the water. 'Let's walk a bit further. I don't suppose there's any food ready yet.'

After having trudged all day through the silent, twilight forest, it was good to hear the birds twittering in the bushes, and feel the warm sun on their faces. They wandered amongst the boulders that littered the water's edge; jumped from rock to rock, and threw pebbles into the pools and little waterfalls that cascaded below them. Scratchit flew in and out of the bushes searching for nuts.

Then, as he stood on an overhanging rock looking down at the water, Andrew heard a slight sound behind him, and at the same time, Scratchit started screeching and scolding, and making a terrible hullabaloo. He turned sharply and saw, not fifteen yards away, a large grey wolf, standing watching him. Plumpearl and her bodyguard had their backs to him a few yards upstream.

'Hey!' shouted Andrew, 'we've got a visitor! Look!' He picked up a stone and took aim. Andrew was a good shot, and it hit the wolf on the side of the head with a crack that he could hear. At the same moment, the dragon, with its eyes almost popping out of its head with fury, wings outstretched, and ferocious jaws snapping, came charging towards him.

The wolf, with its tail between its legs, retreated; and Andrew sat on his boulder and laughed; partly from relief, partly from fright, and partly because the dragon really was a comic sight, with its short legs and ungainly body half-flying, half-jumping over the rocky uneven ground. But Plumpearl, her face white and anxious pointed behind him.

He turned and saw on his left, some thirty yards away, and blocking their path back to Maggins and his camp, a group of twenty or more large wolves standing motionless, eyes following their every move. What to do now? Behind them was the river; in front, a good distance away, the first trees of the forest; and on the right, where the river curved out of sight, both children saw some grey shapes moving swiftly towards them along the river's edge.

'There's only one thing to do!' shouted Andrew, jumping astride the dragon. 'At least we can get to the other bank!'

Plumpearl ran towards him, and climbed up behind. The dragon didn't need any persuading, and with Scratchit flying beside them, they were soon in the air. Looking down Andrew could see the wolves standing in a circle, staring upwards.

'We'll just follow the line of the river,' he shouted against the wind. 'We'll soon see the miners; they must be only a little way along here. Keep an eye open; we're bound to see the smoke of their fire.'

But it wasn't as easy as that. They flew up and down that particular stretch of river again and again, and there wasn't a sign of Maggins, his fire, or his camp.

'He must have gone on without us,' Andrew said. 'He's certainly not down there now.'

At length, they made out a narrow levelled space beside the river, cleared of trees, and clear also of anything else as far as they could see. They circled round for a while, getting gradually lower; and then, as there seemed nothing else to do, landed finally on a broad muddy bank.

'There are footprints in the mud here!' Andrew said at once. 'Huge ones!'

'Dragons probably,' Plumpearl said. 'Look over there!'

On the forest side of the bank on which they had landed, stood a high stone wall, partly overgrown with ivy and creeper, and topped with cruel pointed spikes. Beside it, a broad, roughly turfed walk led over rising ground towards the trees. The wall was high, and anyway there was a deep ditch of water between it and the path, not to mention the spikes. Someone had no intention of it being climbed. So, cautiously, keeping in the shelter of the trees, they followed the path which skirted the wall for about a quarter of a mile, and then disappeared through an iron gate.

Beyond, lay a tangled wilderness of long rank grass, scrubby looking bushes, and more trees; and across the still air came the sound of children's voices. Andrew pushed at the gate. It was locked.

'Let's climb over and see what it's like,' he whispered. 'Perhaps we could find something to eat!'

'I don't think we should. We don't know who lives there.'

'We'll be very careful. But we'd better leave him behind,' he pointed at the dragon, 'that red is so terribly conspicuous! Let's tether him just out of sight, beyond those bushes there.'

'There's no need to tether him. He'll wait if I tell him to; and then if we want him, I'll whistle for him!'

'Right! Now for the gate. Put your foot on the bottom bar, and I'll give you a leg up.'

In spite of her heavy skirts, and the Green Man's cloak, Plumpearl managed quite well, and reached the top of the gate without too much difficulty. Andrew, gripping the metal bars of the gate, was preparing to join her, when he heard a laugh and a rough voice behind them, 'And what do you think you are doing, my fine young lady and gentleman?'

Plumpearl stayed where she was, astride the top of the gate, but Andrew turned to see two soldiers standing looking at him, and grinning. At least he supposed they were soldiers. They wore a kind of rough armour, had helmets on their heads, and carried swords, and the same hooked pikes as the miners. Although, as he stared at them, he realised that what he had taken to be armour, was in fact a dragon skin, with a steel breastplate sewn on to it.

'You're not meant to be outside that wall, are you now?' the soldier said good-humouredly. 'You'd catch it if I were to give you away!' He laughed at them. 'Go on, I've been young myself once! Get down off that gate, and go back to the others, and I won't say anything this time. But don't let me find you here again. It's not safe out in the forest!'

'You're telling me,' muttered Andrew, as they slid down the further side of the wall, and started to run along the path. Plumpearl glanced back at the soldiers who were watching them through the gate. 'They're Dragon People,' she said. 'I wish we hadn't come this way!'

'There wasn't much choice in the end.' Andrew stooped to gather up his cloak. 'I wonder where this leads to? I think we'd better be careful!'

When they were out of sight of the soldiers, they left the path and walked in under the trees. It was an oddly wrecked and trampled landscape. Huge branches lay rotting where they had fallen, broken off from split and jagged stumps; and between them, numerous small fires smouldered and smoked. The trees left standing, their lower trunks smooth and bare of branches, were immensely tall, and the shadows beneath them dense and black.

After five minutes or so, they emerged from the trees, to

find themselves in a dark broken-looking shrubbery which bordered the path. From here, on the far side of a broad expanse of rough turf, they could see an irregular line of low, almost black buildings; and protruding above the trees, stone towers at a higher level than the rest. There was something familiar about the whole place; the black sunken buildings, and stubby conical towers sticking up from the trees. Andrew had the strongest feeling he had seen it all before. But of course that was impossible.

'Where do you think we are?' he whispered.

'I'm not sure . . . can you see what's on that flag up there?'

'Something . . . black? . . . No, I can't.'

The shouts and cries of children were easy to hear now; small figures rushed across the grass before them, and from the path came the clatter of feet running wildly. Many of the children had toy swords and spears, with which they hacked and stabbed at each other in a very realistic fashion.

'Are they really fighting?' Andrew said, raising his head for a better view, 'or is it a game? No, I think they are having a mock battle. It's quite fierce though, isn't it?' Plumpearl was about to say something, when there was a sudden rustling in the bushes, some twigs cracked beside them, and a boy's face appeared smiling mischievously.

'Hiding or finding?' he whispered, holding the branches down with a small sword.

'Er – hiding,' Andrew replied. The boy nodded, and put his finger to his lips.

'They won't find us here,' he said; but Andrew hardly heard him. He was staring at the boy's hand. The nails were very long, and curved like claws; and where the cuff of his sleeve was buttoned round the wrist, he could see that the skin was strangely scaly and segmented. The boy turned and looked at him again. His eyes were a light, bright green; and although he was smiling in a pleasant enough manner, Andrew shuddered. Even his teeth are sharp and pointed, like dragon's teeth, he thought.

At that moment, not very far away, a bell began to ring. The boy jumped to his feet at once. 'Food!' he said. 'Come – or we will get none,' and he was gone.

Andrew stood up. 'We'd better go with him,' he said. 'Shall we? If there's really something to eat! He didn't seem too unfriendly.'

'I don't think we should. These are all Dragon People, and they are always unreliable. Anyway – I don't like the look of this place!'

'Nor do I,' replied Andrew. 'But I don't suppose they'll notice two extra. Look at that lot on the path!'

Before them, a few yards away, moved a shouting, quarrelling crowd of children; and more were approaching. They were dark, with short necks, strong stocky bodies, and rather large heads. Beneath their cloaks, Andrew noticed they were dressed in dragon skins. Most of them had those same disconcerting green glassy eyes and pointed teeth.

'I don't think we should go!' Plumpearl said, clutching at his arm.

But in the end, somewhat nervously, they joined the children on the path; and with their heads well down and their own cloaks fastened tightly round them, walked along, listening to the children's chatter, some of which was in a language that Andrew at least had never heard before.

The low stone building which now came into view had the appearance of either being about to sink into the ground, or of having just risen above it. Apart from the conical towers, it seemed to be largely subterranean; such roofs as they could see being partly covered with turf and rocks.

They followed the press of children through what was

little more than the entrance to a cave, a sort of crack in the ground; and then down a steep flight of stone steps. The air was cold, and smelt of a mixture of damp earth and smoke. They had to be careful where they put their feet, as the light was poor, and the steps were covered with bones and bits of rubbish. The crowd of children obviously knew their way without looking, and rushed down in a noisy stream, pushing and shoving, so that it was a wonder that none of them fell.

The room where they eventually found themselves, and where bowls of food had been laid out on trestle tables, was one of a number opening off a large central hallway – a great paved courtyard, dimly lit, and vaulted over with numerous stone arches. On the far side, splitting the cavernous grey neatly in two, a shaft of light shone from an open door. In the centre of the courtyard, stretched out asleep, its hideous head on its paws, lay a huge dragon chained to a ring in the floor. It was at least twice as big as their own.

'I wonder where we are?' he whispered to Plumpearl beside him. 'Well, it doesn't matter. Let's get something to eat, and then leave as soon as we can.'

There were no chairs, and the other children were already snatching and grabbing at what they could get, tearing the food apart with their fingers, dropping it on the floor, and shouting and talking with their mouths crammed full. Whatever would Gran say to all this? Andrew thought as he watched two boys fighting for possession of a bone under the table.

The food seemed to be mostly huge bones, with lumps of meat attached; but Andrew managed to get what looked like some pieces of chicken, and a few rolls, and the two of them sat silently in the shadow by the wall. Plumpearl ate almost nothing, but wrapped herself up in her cloak, and stared at the children with horrified eyes.

'Put it in your pocket,' murmured Andrew. 'We might be glad of it later.'

He had just about finished, and was trying out the contents of a bottle which someone had put on the floor next to them, when from the open door at the far side of the great hall, came a sudden burst of laughter, and the sound of chairs scraping on stone. Immediately a hush fell on the children, and all faces turned expectantly towards the door. Several men came out into the courtyard, to stand talking and laughing together for a few moments before walking towards the children.

The first man, a short but commanding figure, was dressed entirely in an elaborate suit of dragon scales; jerkin, leggings, shoes – even his black cloak, which hung to the floor in heavy folds, half-covering a corselet of black and silver, was made from a dragon's skin. The head, with its gaping jaws, hung back like a hood; and the leathery tail dragged across the floor behind him. His hair and beard were cropped short, and on his head a magnificent crown flashed and sparkled in the light from the door. His face was broad, handsome even; but with a hooked nose, and coarse pitted skin, which made him look fiercer and more dragon-like than anyone they had yet seen. Two ugly little boys, also in dragon skins and with crowns on their heads, walked beside him; and at a respectful distance, a retinue of courtiers and soldiers followed behind.

'Oh heavens!' Andrew heard Plumpearl gasp beside him. 'It's the King!'

'What? Who?'

'The Black King! – the Black Dragon King!' whispered Plumpearl frantically, and disappeared beneath the nearest table. Andrew sank back against the wall, wishing that he was invisible, yet fascinated against his will by the figure that stood before them.

At this moment, Scratchit, probably because of the smell of food, chose to stick his head out from Andrew's pocket, and from beneath the Green Man's cloak, remarked in a piercing voice, 'Hullo Darling! Dinner-time! Dinner-time!' – something that Mrs Jamieson often said to him.

The benevolent smile on the Dragon King's face vanished instantly; and baring his teeth, he snarled and roared at them so loudly, that Andrew could feel the

69

stones beneath him actually shake. Then he stood before them glowering, hands resting on the heads of his two sons, his stony reptilean eyes flickering from side to side.

No one moved; and Andrew, keeping a tight hold on Scratchit through his cloak, sank even further into the shadows, and gazed at the floor.

After several minutes of ferocious silent glaring, the King began to look less fearsome; one of the courtiers brought him wine, his face relaxed, and he began to smile again.

'Why are the Black Dragon People here?' he asked, sipping his wine.

'To fight! To fight!' yelled the children.

'Who do we all hate?'

'The Red Dragon People!' shrieked the children with glee. It was evidently a game they played often.

'And what are we going to . . .' he didn't even get to the end of the sentence.

'Kill them! Kill them!' yelled the children, stamping their feet. Bloodthirsty little monsters, thought Andrew. The sooner we get out of here the better.

'Kill them! Kill them!' The children banged their fists on the table so that the plates and bowls rattled and jumped. The Dragon King held up his hand.

'I am glad to see all my kinsfolk gathered together under my roof. We may come from different parts of this ancient country of ours, but we are all united in a single purpose. Soon there is to be a great battle! . . .'

'Hurrah!' shouted the children. 'We'll kill them all!'

'A great battle,' continued the King. 'And when we have vanquished the Red Dragon People, then we will go on to Kon – and all its treasures will be ours. May fortune favour our soldiers, your fathers, and us all; and now, I wish you goodnight!'

'Kill them! Kill them!' chanted the children, waving their small swords in the air. 'Kill them all!'

The King nodded his head, and smiled at them again, showing his long pointed dragon teeth; and with his court scurrying behind him, moved slowly back towards the open door. What a horrible place! thought Andrew. The sooner we get away from here the better.

But this was more difficult than he had imagined. Immediately the King had gone, the dragon children left too, chattering with excitement, and several serving girls appeared, and began to clear the tables. Plumpearl resolutely refused to come out from beneath the table, and as Andrew was having considerable difficulty keeping Scratchit in his pocket, he ducked down too. Then Scratchit nipped him through his trousers, and he jumped to his feet in such a hurry that he almost knocked a pile of dishes from the hands of a large woman cleaning the table.

'It's no use you hiding,' she said crossly. 'You're all to go to bed now. Be off with you! How can we ever get our work done?'

'We're just going,' Andrew said politely, dragging Plumpearl to her feet, and half-strangling Scratchit in his pocket.

'I don't remember seeing you before,' the woman said suddenly. 'Where do you come from?'

'We've only just arrived,' Andrew replied quickly, not meeting her eyes. 'Which way do we go?'

'To the right at the top of the stairs, first flight.' She looked at them curiously. 'I thought I hadn't seen you before. What's your name?'

But Andrew and Plumpearl fled, before she could ask any more questions. They ran up one flight of stairs, ignored what must have been the children's quarters, judging by the noise coming from behind a large wooden door, and continued up the second flight. But at the bottom of the third flight, they heard voices above them, and seeing a small passage on their right, turned into it and along to the end. Here, set into the wall, was a shadowy recess, containing what looked like a cupboard door.

The voices of whoever it was on the stairs became louder, passed, and after a while faded.

'What shall we do?' whispered Plumpearl. 'We can't possibly stay here!'

'I know,' Andrew replied. 'But we'd better wait until things quieten down, and then see if we can slip away. I wonder if we could hide in here? It looks like a cupboard.'

On looking inside, however, they found that far from being a cupboard, it opened on to a small gallery or platform, built along one side of an enormously high, large room. A wooden staircase led down from one end of it, and there were balusters at the edge. The light, such as it was, did not reach up to them; so they could not be seen from below. They crept quietly towards the balusters and peeped down into the room.

If you could call it a room, that is! More like a colossal underground cave, its ceiling and further side were lost in darkness; and from a glowing furnace, embedded burning in the floor, even from the cracks between the stones of the floor itself, came a dull orange light. All this was strange enough, but the thing that made them crouch down hastily, their hearts suddenly beating very fast, were the two figures talking together in low voices directly beneath them. One, his broad craggy silhouette unmistakable against the fire, was the Dragon King. The other, sitting in a high-backed golden throne, his furs coloured a pale orange, was the man that Andrew had seen in The Gardens, and for an instant in the mirror of the workbox; the cruel Greyling, the Ice Sorcerer from the North. Stretched on the floor between them, a small dragon dozed.

'Five hundred men, fully armed, and all the animals we shall need,' the King was saying. 'We are ready whenever

72

you give us the word. This time we shall make an end of the Red King, and then for the castle of Kon!'

The Sorcerer smiled, 'And the Gold!' he said softly.

'Yes – of course, the Gold,' agreed the King. There was a pause, and the Greyling was silent.

Then he said, 'We will have to delay our attack on the Red King a little longer. I have the Clock and its Keeper, and I shall have the Key. The Second and the Third Lodges are ours, if not the First – that Green Man is cleverer than I thought. But . . .' and Andrew, for the first time felt really frightened at the fury in his voice, 'that Princess of Kon continues to elude me! I had her safely, where no one in this world could find her. But somehow she has escaped me – *and* she has taken the Guardians of the Clock with her! But I will find her. She cannot hide from me for long.'

'She will try to get back to Kon,' the King said.

'Of course! But we must prevent it! I will not allow my . . . our plans, to be brought to nothing by a mere child.'

Crouching in the shadows of their high platform, the children listened to this conversation as if turned to stone. They hardly dared to breathe, let alone move; and below them the murmur of voices continued, sometimes loud enough for them to hear, sometimes so low, that they could hear nothing.

At length, when they were thinking of trying to retreat towards the door behind them, a soldier entered the room, and bowing very low before the King, said something to him which they could not hear. The King rose to his feet at once.

'I must leave you,' he said. 'There is business to attend to, but I will not be long. I salute you, Great Magician! Remain here, and I will return – perhaps with news that may interest you!' and he stalked out of the room, his scaly cloak sweeping over the floor after him.

The Greyling sat where he was for a while; then getting to his feet, unbuckled a golden sword which hung from a belt under his furs. He removed the belt as well, and placed them both on the table behind him. Suddenly he lifted up his head and laughed, a chilling icy sound, which made the watching children draw together as if for protection.

'Fool!' he called softly, 'Fool! You know nothing! Nothing! The Red King has just as many men! These stupid Dragon People – they are all fools! – but the Black King is the biggest!' He laughed again, and then murmured, 'Kill each other by all means, as many as possible – and the sooner it will all be mine. MINE!' he shouted at the empty room. 'ALL OF IT!'

After this outburst, he returned to his chair, and sat staring into the fire, apparently waiting for the King.

'That's the Sword!' whispered Plumpearl into Andrew's ear. 'On the table. The Magic Sword of Kon!'

'The Sword?' For a moment Andrew did not understand her.

'Without that sword, his power over the Dragon People is lost!'

'Oh you mean . . .' he broke off, as below them the Greyling stirred, and at his feet the dragon raised its head. But after sniffing the air once or twice, it went back to sleep.

They waited for what seemed a lifetime, wondering whether to stay on their precarious perch, or move back to the passage outside. They had decided again to retreat, when the door of the room below burst open, and the Dragon King strode in.

'One of the miners has come to the castle,' he said at once, shouting so they could hear every word. 'They were attacked in the forest and he became separated. He knows nothing of our plans of course! But listen to this!' The

King stood with his arms akimbo, smiling broadly. 'Until a few hours ago, they had the Princess of Kon and a servant with them! What do you think of that? The rest of the miners didn't know her, and wouldn't believe him. But he had seen her once at Kon, and recognised her!'

'Ah!' there was a kind of hissing sigh from the Greyling. '*Now* we have her! – she can't be far off. Where is this man? I must talk to him.' He rose from his chair, and the two of them left the room hurriedly.

The children remained crouched in the dark, staring at each other, wondering what to do. At last Andrew scrambled to his feet.

'Come on!' he whispered. 'I can't stand any more.'

'What about the Sword?' Plumpearl said slowly. 'If we had the Sword . . .' she hesitated, and glanced towards the empty hall beneath them. 'If we had the Sword we could . . .'

'We can't possibly go down there!' Andrew interrupted. 'It would be – well – they might come back at any moment! If we are caught here, neither of us will ever get away.'

But Plumpearl still hesitated. 'And if we leave it?'

'What? – if we leave it?'

'If the Greyling has the Sword, we may escape now, but he will still have the power – over all the Dragon People. We must try and take the Sword with us!'

'Well – I'm not going down. And you mustn't either. We've got to get out of this place at once . . . Plumpearl! . . . Plumpearl! . . . Come back!'

But the Princess had already started towards the stairs at the side of the gallery, which groaned and creaked beneath her weight. As she reached the bottom, the dragon raised its head and watched her for a moment; but only blinked its glass-green eyes, and shifted its position before the fire.

Like a shadow, Plumpearl crept slowly across the huge room, and Andrew held his breath. She looked so tiny in the flickering light, a little fragile doll holding up its cloak and rustling skirts. He had a horrid feeling it should be him down there; and yet he doubted if he could have made himself go. Hurry! What an age she was taking! Ah! – at last, she was there. She had the Sword in her hands, and was coming back. She was halfway across the room. Well – come on! Andrew was trembling with impatience. Why was she just standing there? He glanced towards the door – and saw that it was open; and saw too the unmistakable figure of the Greyling silhouetted against the orange light from without.

7 What Next?

Holding the sword before her, Plumpearl stood staring at the Sorcerer as if caught in a snare. And the Greyling, his white frozen face set in an evil smile, stared back.

'Good evening my dear,' he said at last, entering the room swiftly, and bending to lock the door after him, 'we meet again! How strange! How delightful! There is no one I would rather see – just at this moment.' He stood motionless, looking at her in a way that made Andrew feel sick.

'What are you hoping to do with the – my – sword, I wonder?' he said at last, taking a step towards her.

'It's not yours,' Plumpearl replied fiercely. 'You are a – a thief, just a thief. All you want is the Gold . . .'

'Oh we *are* brave tonight.' There was no mistaking the menace in his voice.

Andrew shivered and closed his eyes. This is the end he thought. How will we ever get to Kon now? Why did I let her go down? I should have done it. If I'd gone, maybe I could have passed myself off as one of the Castle children.

Below him, he heard the Greyling gabbling and screaming like a mad old woman. Suddenly there was a loud clang, as if of metal on stone. The Sword! thought Andrew, what's happened? Has she dropped it? He peeped once more through the banisters, and drew in his breath sharply. The Sword was on the stone floor; but except for the dragon still dozing by the fire, the Sorcerer was alone. Before him, where a moment earlier Plumpearl had stood, lay a small grey sack. Of Plumpearl there wasn't a sign. Where had she got to?

The answer came soon enough, as the Greyling, still laughing wildly, scooped up the sack, and held it above his head. 'I'm taking you back, my dear!' he cried triumphantly. 'No one escapes the Greyling! No one! Now that I have you again – everything is mine. MINE! Who can prevent it? The fools! – they'll never find you, not where I have hidden you!'

He opened the sack a fraction, and looked into it. 'Why do you flutter so, little bird? Soon you will be back in your beautiful silver cage. Or shall we make it a golden one this time?' He threw the sack over his shoulder, and laughed again so that Andrew's heart seemed to freeze in his body at the sound. Then, as he had in The Gardens, he simply vanished from sight; only this time he was careful to take the Sword and the sack with him. And except for a faint echo of laughter reverberating round the great hall, and the dragon before the fire, Andrew and Scratchit were alone.

For a while he sat on in the dark, biting his nails, and wondering what to do. What a mess! His grandmother completely vanished – not to mention Miss Shooter, and now the only person with the faintest idea of where to look for them whisked away from under his nose. Poor Plumpearl! She was in that sack again without a doubt. He should have stopped her going down. Well, it was too late now. But he'd have to try and find her; he was the only one who knew what had happened.

It was difficult to know where to start. What was it the Greyling had said? – 'I'm taking you back!' Back where? 'Hide you again!' – what did that mean? Where had she been hidden before? The only place he knew about for pretty well certain was the birdcage in that horrible Vanishing Trick in Mr Grottel's shop. Was he taking her there? He had mentioned a cage, and Mr Grottel was somehow involved in all this. Why had he been so keen to get hold of the Dragon Clock? And the work-box had come from him! They must be in it together. In fact, the more Andrew considered it, the more obvious it seemed. 'Grottel and Greyling – Partners.' Yes, that was it! They were in it together for the Gold! Mr Grottel had told him he expected to be rich soon; although his chances of getting his hands on any gold, after what Andrew had heard that night in the Dragon Castle, did not seem to be very great.

Taking her back *again*! It would be difficult for any of these strange Forest People to find their way to Mr Grottel's shop; almost as difficult as it is for me, thought Andrew. But I'll have a try. There seemed very little chance he could make his way to Kon alone. So what else could he do?

'Come on!' he said, as much to himself as Scratchit, who was beginning to fidget, 'we're leaving!'

As quietly as he could, he ran towards the stairs, and after climbing several more flights came out on to an open flat roof, surrounded by irregular pointed battlements. Ahead was a narrow circular tower, its entrance directly opposite him, and inside more steps curving upwards. But before he had had a chance to see how far he was from the ground, he heard voices coming from the stairs behind him. Andrew ran into the tower and began once more to climb. I'll hide up here until it's all clear he thought.

It seemed as if the steep cramped little steps would never end; and he was breathless and giddy when he finally reached the top. Thankfully he threw himself down, and lying on his stomach squinted out from between the narrow slits cut in the protecting wall.

He was quite unprepared for the vast panorama which lay below. Facing him, and low in the sky, a huge orange sun hovered, and beneath it, spread out like an undulating sea, stretched the forest: green, dark, peaceful, no hint of the dangers within. Between the trees, the river glinted and shone; and to the north, where the forest ended, a wide rocky plain – which Andrew suddenly realised, was mostly snow and ice – extended to the horizon. Beyond this again, mountains showed, their tops tinged with pink.

For a moment Andrew forgot his predicament, and lay gazing at the forest and distant hills, and the pink and golden clouds drifting over him. Then he saw something that made him raise his head sharply. On the horizon, and rising above the clouds, almost as if hanging in the sky itself, were the delicate outlines of a vast Palace: pinnacles, turrets, and a host of towers and battlements, soaring spires and buttresses, all glowing red and gold in the evening light.

That must be Kon! – thought Andrew. Goodness! It's miles away. I'll never get there alone.

He wriggled forward to look down again at the forest; and then at the flat roof from which he had just come. He could see that actually it wasn't very far from the ground, but on it now, two soldiers paced up and down. Those must have been the voices he had heard. No good going down there at the moment.

Some way over to the left of the tower, and above the trees, what he took to be some large birds circled idly round on a current of rising air. But there was something odd about them. What was it? One of them came a little nearer, and then swooped low above the river; and he saw that they were not birds at all, but dragons flying with their tails looped up, and their necks stretched out, exactly like the dragons on the work-box. And the stone towers sticking up out of the trees! He knew suddenly why they were familiar. He had seen them before! – in the painting on the Dragon Clock! But what about the figure under the trees? Was that the Greyling? And Plumpearl? – had she reappeared, only to vanish again? Well, at least he knew where he was, although it didn't seem as if it was going to help much.

He decided to wait until it was dark, and then see if he could climb down the castle wall into the forest, and find the dragon. It was tempting to use the little mirror, and just fade back into his own safe, ordinary world. But where would that land him he wondered? It didn't seem as safe as all that. And anyway if he was going back to Verbena Lodge, he must have the dragon with him for speed. I wonder if the Green Man can see me here he thought, twisting the ring on his thumb, and looking away hastily as the eye gazed up at him.

He waited, watching the sun sink below the horizon, and the grey shadows come creeping over the sky from the north. At length, when it was quite dark, and very cold, he stood up, preparing to creep down the stairs. But at that moment he heard the beating of powerful wings above him, and out of the sky came the red dragon, four legs outstretched, to land beside him with scarcely a sound. How had he known where to come? The Green Man *can* see me he thought; and felt suddenly comforted. He scrambled up on to the dragon's back, and in seconds they were away, flying at speed across the silent forest.

After they had been flying for about twenty minutes, the moon rose, and Andrew caught a glimpse of the river below. He pointed into the dark beneath them, and obediently the dragon skimmed over the tops of the trees, until they found a clearing in which to land. Immediately they were on the ground, Andrew pulled his cloak around them both, held up the mirror and gazed into it. Almost at once the forest landscape faded, became transparent, and then vanished altogether, and another entirely different took its place.

Andrew replaced the mirror in his pocket carefully, and stared about him wondering where he was. Although it was still dark, the moon shone faintly, and to his relief he could see that a wide sweeping hillside had taken the place of the trees. From not very far away came the sound of a ship hooting, and then some other vessel's answering signal. He was still near a river.

'Morning Darling!' croaked Scratchit inside his jacket, and Andrew laughed. In spite of all the awful things that had happened, he felt better in his own familiar world. He wrapped his cloak about him, lay down beside the dragon, and the three of them slept until dawn.

When Andrew awoke, it took him a little while to remember the events of the preceding night. But once he had remembered he sat up with a start.

'Come on everyone,' he said, getting to his feet. 'We'll walk down to that river, and see if we can find out where we are.'

Actually, it wasn't very difficult. They followed a sandy path, which led downhill towards the water, and they hadn't gone very far, when they came across a large wooden notice board which said – GRAVESEND FERRY – and then a lot of small print, which Andrew didn't bother to read.

'Gravesend,' he said, half to himself, and half to Scratchit. 'Well! That must be the Thames down there then!' If he had been wearing a cap, he would have thrown it into the air. 'I know where we are! Do you see? We just have to follow the river – but in which direction I wonder? Let me think!'

He stood looking at the sun, which was just beginning to rise above the misty horizon; then he squatted down, and drew a circle on the hard sand of the path. The sun rises in the east, he thought, and the opposite of east is west. He tried to imagine a map of England, with the Thames pouring forth into the sea. He knew that the sea on that side was called the East Coast. So east would be quite the wrong direction. Better try for the west. He pointed in what he hoped was a westerly direction, and climbed on to the dragon.

'Go on! – fly!' called Andrew encouragingly, kicking his heels into the animal's side. 'Over there; towards the west!'

Scratchit rose into the air above them; and after a moment the dragon followed, springing upwards in one great bound; his huge wings beating rhythmically, lifting them higher and higher, in an ever ascending spiral. Andrew, with his arms clasped tightly round the animal's neck, and his cloak billowing out behind him, gazed in wonder at London spread out beneath them bathed in the golden light from the sun. It was easy to see the river shining between the mist, and they flew west-wards above it, until Andrew's fingers were so stiff and cold, that he knew that if he lost his balance, he would not be able to hold on.

They must have been travelling for about an hour or more, when he saw something below them, that he was sure he recognised. A huge grey block of a building, with hundreds of windows, and a Union Jack on the top, set in its own green gardens and park. Buckingham Palace! That wasn't too far from the Bayswater Road; he knew, because he had once walked there with Gran. Leaning forward, he patted the dragon's neck, and pointed downwards.

He had hoped that the dragon would lessen its speed, circle round for a bit to let him get his bearings, and then somehow make for Verbena Gardens. But no such luck!

It tipped itself forward, spread out its great wings, and sailed downwards at a tremendous speed. Andrew closed his eyes, and held on, praying that they would land somewhere suitable. It wasn't too bad. They came down at the bus stop, just in front of the Albert Hall. But although there was no one about, and very little traffic, Andrew felt very conspicuous and he crossed the road into the park quickly. We'll walk he thought. I'll find my way easily from here.

It was further than he had remembered, but he was glad to be on familiar ground, and whistled cheerfully as they walked along. He wondered what he would find at Verbena Lodge? Perhaps his grandmother was back?

They had reached the further side of the park, crossed the Bayswater Road, and were turning into Verbena Gardens, when they almost bumped into a large policeman strolling along as if he owned the place.

'Morning,' Andrew said, dodging past him, with the dragon following behind. 'Nice day.'

'Hey!' the policeman said. 'Where are you going – with, er – that? What is it anyway?' he turned to examine the dragon more closely.

'A – a – red – er – Iguana,' Andrew said hopefully. 'We're taking him to the Zoo this afternoon. Getting too big to take around now.'

'I should think he jolly well is,' the policeman said, taking his helmet off and replacing it. 'Where do you live then?'

'Verbena Lodge.'

'Oh yes, Mrs Jamieson.' He looked at the dragon again with eyes that said of course Mrs Jamieson would keep a thing like that. 'You've got the old lady's parrot, too, I see.'

'Yes,' said Andrew. 'I've just been taking them all for – a – er – walk. We're going to have breakfast now.

Goodbye!' and he left the policeman staring after them with a disapproving expression on his face, and ran as fast as he could towards Verbena Lodge. The front door was shut, but he knew where the back-door key was kept; and after collecting two days' milk, a sliced loaf and six eggs, he let himself, Scratchit and the dragon into the kitchen.

8 Mr Grottel Again

Andrew was famished, and before thinking about anything else, he set to, and made himself a gigantic breakfast: baked beans, scrambled eggs, toast, and an outsized mug of cocoa. After that, he considered his two companions. Scratchit sat hunched on the end of the table, his feathers ruffled and greasy looking, his eyes half closed, the picture of misery; and the dragon must have been dreadfully hungry, because while Andrew was searching for the tin of nuts which he knew must be in the larder somewhere, the great beast suddenly stretched up its head, and wolfed down the half loaf, and remaining eggs – shells, containers, and all – which Andrew had left on the kitchen table. Then he lay on the floor, rolling his eyes, and looking pathetic, just like a dog.

I don't really know what he eats, Andrew thought; but I suppose I'd better not let him get too hungry! And after he had chopped up a rather withered apple, and given it to Scratchit with the nuts and some water, he opened two large tins of steak and onions, poured three pints of milk into a basin, and put it on the floor. Then he set off on a tour of the house.

It was unnervingly quiet for Verbena Lodge; and he jumped when the window of the pantry rattled in a sudden gust of wind. The clocks still aren't going, he thought, and . . . Why are all the coats in the hall on the floor? And the umbrellas? How untidy everything is! He opened the drawing-room door, and looked inside. It was a shambles. Pictures askew on the walls, curtains dangling half on their rails, half off; the desk was open, and all Mrs Jamieson's papers had spilled on to the floor. The books in the shelves had been pulled out, and lay in disordered heaps, in company with newspapers, cushions, clocks, ornaments, and heaven knows what else. It seemed very much as if someone had been searching for something. Andrew had never seen such a mess; and it was the same all over the house.

After having examined every room, he went round once more, and fastened the catches on the windows; and before going downstairs, he locked and bolted the door which led up to the attic. Nobody could get in now, without smashing their way in! As far as he could judge, the only things obviously missing were the work-box – which he didn't expect to find – and the Dragon Clock. Not surprising in the circumstances; although what was the point of ransacking the house for a huge thing like that? It must be something small they're looking for – maybe this? he thought, taking the key of the Dragon Clock out of his pocket. Whoever had the clock, probably wanted the key.

From St Marks on the other side of Verbena Gardens, he heard eleven o'clock strike. Time was passing. He stood for a moment irresolute, trying to remember the Greyling's words. What was it he had said? – 'I'm taking you back' – and he had actually mentioned the birdcage. Well! – it was worth a try. But how to get into the shop, without Mr Grottel himself breathing down his neck? And the house at the back where he lived, he'd have to look there too. He glanced at the Green Man's ring, and the disconcerting eye gazed back, but without giving him any ideas. Andrew twiddled the ring on his thumb, and looked at the dragon asleep under the kitchen table. Somehow he must remove Mr Grottel temporarily from his shop. But how? Suddenly he smiled, went out into the hall, and took down the telephone book E–K, practically the only thing in the house that wasn't on the floor.

He could hear the telephone ringing at the other end; and then a voice, a quite unmistakable voice, said 'Yes? – Grottel speaking. Can I help you?'

'Good morning,' piped Andrew, in a high unnatural falsetto, 'I have a rather valuable clock I wish to sell. Would you be interested? I am – er – I am leaving on a long journey this afternoon, and I want to make all the – er – the – arrangements, before I go. I believe you buy clocks?'

'Yes Madam – we do buy clocks from time to time. What kind is it?'

'Antique . . . very old,' Andrew said. He was finding it hard to stop himself from laughing. 'Eighteenth century – rather valuable.' There was a pause.

'Where do you live Madam? If it's near, I could come round in the lunch hour. What is the address?'

'Seventeen Kensington Park Terrace – just off Kensington Park Gardens,' Andrew said, without a moment's hesitation. 'Mrs Andrews.'

'Oh yes! Walking distance. Thank you, I shall be very interested to see your clock Mrs Andrews. Shall we say shortly after twelve-thirty?'

'Yes. All right, that will do fine. Goodbye!' Andrew put down the receiver, giggling. It would take Mr Grottel at least twenty minutes to walk to Kensington Park Gardens; another ten minutes looking for Kensington Park Terrace, which didn't exist, and then twenty minutes back. At the very least, he had forty minutes, if not an hour in which to search that crummy little shop round the corner from top to bottom! He grinned at the ring on his thumb, and winked at it; and, so much had happened which was strange and inexplicable, that when, without any doubt the stone eye winked back, he hardly gave it a thought.

Still smiling, Andrew went back into the kitchen, and rummaging in the larder, found a good supply of biscuits, some stale fruit cake, and a large slab of cooking chocolate: this time, he had no intention of being hungry. He put them into a canvas satchel that belonged to Miss Shooter, and went upstairs to fetch his compass. The Gardens looked so quiet and peaceful from his bedroom window, that for a moment he was tempted to stay where he was, and not go careering off once more on another wild-goose chase. But he forced himself back into the kitchen, and slinging the satchel over his shoulder, buttoned a rather reluctant Scratchit into his jacket. He was ready. Oh! – What about the dragon dozing on the kitchen floor? I can't take that great thing with me, he thought, I'll have half London after me!

'You stay there!' he said as the dragon looked up. 'I'll come back for you – I hope!' He glanced round the room to see if he had forgotten anything; then let himself out of the back door, locking it after him.

The dairy opposite Mr Grottel's shop was the perfect place for observation; it had an area at the side, on whose steps he could stand, with only his eyes above ground level.

Andrew studied the Magic Shop carefully. 'Grottel and Greyling – Magic Shop' was painted above the dusty glass of the window. Well! That's plain enough, thought Andrew. He had never realised before that, sandwiched between the shop and the block of flats next door, was an extremely narrow passage, which normally you hardly noticed, unless you happened to be looking straight at it, as he was now. That must be where his front door is, thought Andrew.

Promptly at twelve-fifteen, Mr Grottel appeared in his hat and coat, and let himself out of the shop, after having put a notice in his window which said – 'Closed for Lunch'. Andrew watched him lock the door, try it to make sure it was secure, and then walk away briskly in the direction of the Park. Andrew waited until he was out of sight, and then ran across the road.

The door to the shop was closed, of course, so the only hope was the alley. It was very narrow, not much more than a crack between two buildings, ending in a small, dank courtyard. One side of this was the steep towering mass of the flats, the other, the side of Mr Grottel's shop; and the third, facing him, a blank wall with a brown door in it. In the top of the door was an open fanlight. That *must* be Grottel's front door! thought Andrew. Where else could it lead to? With luck the fanlight was just about big enough for him to squeeze through. He took a running leap at the door, pulled himself up, and in a moment had dropped down on the other side, pushing Scratchit before him.

He was in a gloomy narrow hallway, with a staircase leading out of it, and to the left a door painted green. Cautiously Andrew pushed it open, and at once found himself standing behind the narrow curtain at the back of the shop. He stood gazing round at all the familiar objects, hoping for some clue, some sign that would tell him that he was on the right track; but he could see nothing that was different from how it generally was. I'll go back into the house, and see if I can find anything there, he thought.

Once in the hall, he ran up the stairs to the first landing where two doors faced each other. He opened first one and then the other, staring in disbelief at each room in turn. They were both entirely empty. Bare walls and

floorboards; nothing else at all. And it was the same on each of the three floors. Every room in the house was completely empty, no furniture, no curtains, no pictures, nothing. Just a shell, thought Andrew, running down the stairs, how extraordinary! But he must live somewhere! Then, as he stood in the hall, wondering where else he could look, he heard the Dragon Clock strike the half hour. It was unmistakable, he would have known it anywhere. But from which direction did it come? It sounded almost as if it was beneath him. He went to the side of the stairs, and saw a small triangular door set into the wall below the staircase, which he hadn't noticed before. Inside were two shallow steps, and a well-lit, tiled passage. At the end of this, at a slightly lower level, another door. To where? Probably a cellar, thought Andrew. He looked at his watch. Just half past; he should have at least half an hour before Mr Grottel came back.

With his mouth a little dry, and his heart beating uncomfortably fast, he stepped through and ran to the end of the passage. Perhaps this will be empty too, he thought.

But although it was rather dark, what light there was filtering in from a grating in the ceiling, he could see at once that, far from being empty, it was literally crammed to the roof with objects: books, jewellery, furniture, mirrors, and thousands, perhaps millions, of clocks. They were everywhere, on every available surface; on the floor, on shelves, desks, tables, even hanging from the ceiling. And in the centre of all this, above a small table, was the Dragon Clock, without its dragons of course, but still measuring out the time with its slow unhurried beat. Leaning against the table he saw the Sword, the golden Sword of Kon; and on the floor beside it – a birdcage. Inside the cage, pressed up against the bars, was a small golden bird with grey markings round its neck. He took a step forward, and then stopped. Someone was standing on the far side of the room. In the half light it was difficult to see who.

Andrew stood transfixed, staring horrified at the figure in the corner. Then the caged bird gave a harsh cry, and dashed its wings against the bars of its cage – and broke the illusion. It wasn't a person, but a coat on a peg in the wall, and on it, hanging from the same peg, was one of Mr Grottel's masks, which was so extremely life-like, that anybody could be forgiven for thinking it was someone real.

Heavens, he thought, that gave me a turn! I must get out of here, before I lose my wits completely. The bird croaked again, and he opened the cage. Immediately it flew towards the Dragon Clock, and perched there, bowing and dipping its sleek little head, as if watching the hands of the clock. At the same moment, Scratchit slipped from his shoulder, and flew towards the clock, where he too perched, staring down at the face, as he had so many times before.

Andrew's first impulse was to grab them both, and rush out. He felt thoroughly uncomfortable in this dark, crowded room. Supposing Mr Grottel took a bus back? He must hurry. But it was no .se charging out with poor Plumpearl in that state; and he had no idea how to get her back to her proper shape. He stared at the little bird desperately. What should he do? Then he remembered the Dragon Clock, and the first time he had seen Plumpearl as she really was. He took the key out of his pocket, unlocked the glass case, and started to move the large hand round, until one o'clock chimed. He moved the hand again, and two o'clock boomed forth. By the time he had got to ten o'clock, he was trembling with fright and impatience. Grottel will hear this from a mile away, he thought, as the clock began to chime eleven. Now – twelve o'clock! Would it work?

Andrew gazed at the little bird intently. One, two, three . . . Nothing was happening. Or was it? He couldn't decide. Four . . . five . . . six . . . Yes! He could see again the change beginning. The bird was taller, bigger, its beak disappearing, its eyes getting larger. Seven . . . eight . . . nine . . . Andrew watched fascinated, as rapidly the bird changed before his eyes. It was almost complete; the beautiful shining clothes were almost there, the feathers gradually fading, slipping away. The last solemn notes sounded, and Plumpearl stood before him once more; her golden dress a little crumpled and torn, but smiling and well, and above all a girl, not a bird.

'Thank goodness!' Andrew said with intense relief. 'I thought it wasn't going to work!'

'How did you . . .?' began Plumpearl. But Andrew interrupted her.

'Come on!' he said. 'We must get away at once! I don't think we have very much time.' He looked at his watch. It was a quarter to one.

'How did you find this place?'

'Never mind – I'll tell you everything later.' He took her hand, called to Scratchit, and they ran towards the door. Andrew opened it, and they stood listening for any sound from without. They were about to start down the passage, when in the hall at the far end, they both heard the rattle of keys, and then the front door slam.

'Quick! Hide! – behind here!' Andrew pointed towards the wall behind the door, where a collection of coats hung limply from their pegs. They ducked underneath them, and stood waiting, scarcely daring to breathe. Suddenly Andrew remembered Scratchit! Oh Christmas! he thought, he's loose out there. If only he keeps quiet.

They heard quick light footsteps along the passage, and an exclamation as Mr Grottel came into the room.

'Who's been in here?' The whispered words were only a few feet from them. And then – 'She's gone! Oh – he'll kill me! She's gone! Who has taken her?' The voice was full of – not anger, but fear – or so Andrew thought. As if bewitched, he stared through a gap in the coats which hid them. He could see Mr Grottel quite plainly, or rather his back, bending over the Dragon Clock. There was complete silence, and Andrew realised suddenly that the slow ticking of the huge clock no longer dominated the room: it had stopped! There was a fresh wail from Mr Grottel.

'The Clock! The Clock!' he sounded desperate. 'What shall I do? I'll never get it going again!' – and in fury – 'Who *has* been in here?'

Andrew waited petrified, clutching Plumpearl's hand. It seemed as if they must be found. He was sure their feet were showing. At that moment, from the very far end of the room, behind the screens, old tables, cupboards and clutter of books and clocks, he heard Scratchit's voice, low and chuckling – 'Are you a good boy? Are you a good boy?' – and then silence. Andrew had taught him to say this, and at any other time he would have been delighted; but now he froze behind the coats feeling sick and frightened.

Mr Grottel stood up. Scratchit's voice seemed to startle him. 'Who's that?' He glanced at the half-open door, looked again at the clock, then walked away from them down the centre of the room.

Andrew parted the coats cautiously. Nothing moved – Mr Grottel had vanished temporarily, obscured by the jungle of furniture at the end of the room. But no doubt he would be back!

'Come on!' Andrew stepped out from behind the coats. 'This may be our only chance!'

'What about Scratchit?' but as Plumpearl whispered the question Scratchit darted above their heads, and flitted out through the open door, into the passage beyond. Andrew snatched up the Sword, and the children followed, racing after the parrot into the dark little hall. There was a shout from behind; but the key was still in the keyhole of the triangular door. Quickly Andrew locked it; and pulling open the front door without any difficulty, they rushed down the alley. In the street they stopped for a moment; and Scratchit flew up on to the roof of the shop, and then took off in the direction of Verbena Lodge.

'He thinks I'm going to put him in my pocket again I suppose!' Andrew said. 'Well – he'll have to go. He can find his way home quite easily from here. We can't wait around for him now!'

They started running again, and soon were half a mile down the Bayswater Road.

'What about the dragon?' the Princess said, when at last they stopped for breath.

'He's at Verbena Lodge – with Scratchit by now, I expect.' Andrew laughed. 'They can keep each other company.'

'Couldn't we travel with him?'

'I don't think we should go back there at the moment. We'll have to deal with him later. Anyway I've had enough of travelling through that awful forest. We're going a different way this time.'

'Where are we going then?'

'To Gravesend and across the river.' He took the little mirror from his pocket. 'At least that's what we'll try and do. I can't imagine how we will manage if this doesn't work. But I rather think it will.'

They walked across the park to Victoria Bus Station; and there Andrew enquired about getting to Gravesend. There wasn't a coach for an hour, so they wandered down on to the embankment, and as the Princess was hungry, Andrew fished in his pocket, and produced what was left of his birthday money.

'I should think I've enough for a cup of tea and a bun each,' he said. In fact it was enough for a couple of sausages as well; and Plumpearl had Andrew's bun as he was still full up from breakfast.

'And what's she supposed to be?' the proprietor of the coffee-stall enquired, eyeing Plumpearl's magnificent if crumpled golden dress.

'A Princess,' Andrew replied absently, as Plumpearl stared at the man without understanding.

'I see,' the man said. 'Where are you off to then? Buckingham Palace?'

'Gravesend,' Andrew said, 'on the coach.'

'That's a long way!' The man leaned over to give them their tea. Andrew nodded, and then murmured half to himself, 'That's only the beginning I'm afraid. Still, it's better than the forest, with all those wolves and things.'

The coffee-stall man laughed. 'Oh yes – you want to watch out for the wolves!' And as Plumpearl and Andrew walked away towards the Coach Station, he shook his head and muttered '— Children nowadays! You never know what they're up to.'

At Gravesend, they walked along the towpath towards the ferry; and Andrew looking upwards from the raised embankment, recognised the sloping hillside where he had spent the previous night.

'Here we are,' he said, 'that's your country over there!' He waved his hand in the direction of the smudged, flat land, and maze of smoking chimneys that lay spread out before them on the further side of the river. 'As far as I can remember, your home was in the north wasn't it?' He took his compass out of his pocket. 'If we keep walking in that direction' – he pointed before him – 'we should get there.'

'Where?'

'Kon – the Palace, your home – it's over there!'

'So far? Do you think we can walk that far?' the Princess said.

'Of course we can. We'll have to; buses don't follow compasses. Anyway, I've hardly any money left. If you want to get home, we'll have to walk. There's no other way!'

Plumpearl smiled. 'I'll walk a hundred miles to get home,' she said. You may have to, thought Andrew, but he said nothing, and they continued along the path, until they reached the ferry.

By the time they had crossed the river, it was five o'clock. They had had a rest on the coach however, so started walking in good spirits. At about seven they sat down on a seat at the side of the road, and Andrew took out the slab of cooking chocolate, and the sausages that he had wrapped in his handkerchief.

'Are you sure you know where you are going?' Plumpearl said at last, licking her fingers. Andrew took out his compass.

'North,' he said, 'due north. Tell me – the Palace of Kon, you said it was a day's journey from, from . . .'

'From that place by the river where we saw the wolves,' interrupted Plumpearl. 'Yes, about a day's journey.'

'Walking or flying?'

'Walking.'

'I thought so. Good.' Andrew rose to his feet. 'If we just keep going – we'll get there; or near, anyway. And then we'll think what to do.'

And so they walked, on and on interminably. Through busy streets with shops on either side; squares and quiet avenues. Past large houses, cottages, schools, churches, parks, with children's swings and roundabouts beyond the railings. Through vast factory estates, warehouses and the deserted alleys between them; then more streets. Once they had to cross an enormous concrete highway, with cars rushing past them in an endless stream. Plumpearl wanted to stay and watch them, but Andrew hurried her along. It began to get dark, and the street lights came on. It was a clear, brilliant night, with an infinite company of stars twinkling above them. Andrew wished he could remember how to navigate by the stars, but he couldn't. So from time to time he took out his compass to make sure they were still travelling north.

At last, after they had been walking for several hours and Andrew, though he would not have admitted it, was beginning to feel terribly footsore and sleepy, the Princess suddenly sat down by the side of the road.

'I can't go any further,' she said in a faint voice. 'I must have a rest!'

'Well – we can't rest here,' Andrew said. 'If anybody sees us, they'll wonder what we are doing. People are so funny.' He looked down the road anxiously. It was an ordinary enough street – thousands like it all over London – but something at the end of it gave him an idea.

The road menders had been at work. There was a jagged hole in the road, with trestles and planks and red lights all round it; and on the pavement by the side was a little red and white shelter, the opening tied up with tapes like a tent.

'Just the place!' Andrew said. 'We can rest in there. No one will see us, and we'll leave before anyone comes in the morning.'

Inside the shelter, it was too good to be true. There were two benches on either side of it; some tarpaulins, and a pile of overalls on the floor. There was even a tarry old coat hanging from inside the roof.

'It's a bit smelly,' Andrew said, wrinkling his nose, 'but it will have to do.' He folded up the overalls for pillows,

100

put the coat over the Princess, and the tarpaulin over himself, and soon they were stretched out on the benches fast asleep.

In the morning, the sun woke them early, and they were on their way before anyone was stirring. After they had been walking for an hour or so, they bought a pint of milk from a friendly milkman. It was the last of the money.

'You're up early!' the milkman said. 'Who's she? The Queen of Sheba?'

'That's right!' Andrew smiled. 'I'm just taking her home.'

'Oh! You've got a goodish way to go then,' the milkman laughed, dumping down an empty crate of bottles with a crash.

'Yes, I'm afraid we have. Never mind, we'll get there.'

''Course you will!' the milkman jumped on his float, and started it up. 'Ta-rah! Sorry I don't take in Sheba on my round!'

The milk tasted fresh and creamy, and they had a bit of fruit cake each, which stale and dry as it was, went down all right. It just depends how hungry you are, thought Andrew, not for the first time. Refreshed, they set off once more.

The sun climbed slowly into the sky above them. It was going to be a hot day. People began to appear in the streets; first on their way to work; later on, mothers going shopping, housewives cleaning their front steps and shaking rugs from windows.

Andrew was wondering for the hundredth time how much further they had to go, when he noticed that the land was beginning to slope upwards. In fact, without realising it they were plodding up quite a steep hill. Perhaps that was why he felt so tired.

'What's it like round this Palace of yours?' he said,

stopping for a moment to take a stone out of his shoe. 'I mean – the countryside? Is it a friendly sort of place, or are there dragons there too?'

'Usually the black dragons don't come out on to the plain,' the Princess said. 'Mostly they keep to the forest, because they can be seen so easily. There is a flat open plain all round the Palace; and anybody can be seen. There are red dragons on it sometimes; and the miners go backwards and forwards of course. But we know them.'

'How big is this plain?'

'Very wide and big. Every year the trees come a little nearer, but we send soldiers and cut them down. Then we can always see who is on the plain. We don't go into the forest very often.'

'And this plain – it stretches all round the Palace, does it?'

'Yes – although now the northern side is covered in ice.'

'So if we were on the plain, we'd probably be all right, even if we were far away?'

'Whatever it is, and however small, if it is on the plain, we can see it from the Palace.'

'Mmm. I wonder if we are getting anywhere near it,' murmured Andrew.

He was beginning to think he'd been over-optimistic in imagining that just by setting off in a vaguely northerly direction from some point near the Dragon King's stronghold, they would as a matter of course, arrive at the Palace of Kon. It was true he had caught a glimpse of it yesterday; and as far as he could remember, it lay due north from the tower. But had they been walking in the right direction? On the other hand, something as clearly visible as that wonderful red and gold building, must be pretty conspicuous from a good way off. So if they were walking more or less in the right direction, surely there was a good chance that they'd see it?

'It all depends if we recognise it when we get there, I suppose,' he said at last, putting his shoe on.

They were sitting on the kerb in a wide tree-lined avenue, with solid-looking houses set in large gardens on either side of the road. Andrew felt very tired and a bit headachy in the hot sun. Beside him the Princess yawned.

'How much further do you think it is?' she said, holding up her slippers to show him the holes in both.

'I don't know. Not too far I hope.'

'I'm thirsty,' Plumpearl remarked, after a long silence.

'So am I. I suppose we could go and ask for a drink in one of these houses!' Andrew looked doubtfully at the gate behind them. It had a small china notice on it which said, 'No Hawkers or Callers. Beware of the Dog. Tradesmen right-hand entrance.'

'What's a hawker?' asked Plumpearl, as Andrew read it out.

'A hawker is a – a – well, it's a sort of . . .' he really couldn't be bothered to explain. He shielded his eyes from the sun, and gazed at another group of travellers walking slowly towards them up the avenue.

'A hawker is a – a – a . . .' They looked tired too. An elderly man with a bandage round his head, and an old beret stuck on top of that, was in front, leading a string of donkeys. At the end of the line, a few boys followed behind with sticks, tapping the donkeys from time to time to keep them on the move.

'I wish we could ride on those!' Plumpearl sighed. 'I wonder where they are going?'

'Probably to give people rides at some fair,' Andrew said, resting his chin on the hilt of the Sword, and studying the little procession as it moved past. He had the oddest feeling that he had seen the man before; and quite recently too. At a fair perhaps? – Or on Hampstead Heath? He knew there were donkeys on the Heath in the summer; he had often ridden on them. And yet, there was something about the man himself; his slow slightly rolling gait, big head, short legs and powerful broad shoulders that reminded him of someone. But he couldn't think who.

Suddenly Andrew leapt to his feet. 'Of course! It's Maggins!' he shouted.

'Maggins – where? That's not Maggins!' Plumpearl said mystified. 'That man is entirely different. He's – well, he's someone else!'

'Yes! Different *here*. But there's still something the same. Hey!' shouted Andrew, 'MAGGINS! MAGGINS!' but the man with the donkeys did not turn round.

'No – of course! – He wouldn't be called Maggins here. So he wouldn't answer! Quick, where's that mirror thing?'

Fumbling in his excitement and haste, Andrew felt in his trouser pockets. In his inside and jacket pockets, and again in his trouser pockets. It wasn't there. He searched all through his pockets again slowly and methodically; but it was no use. It must have slipped out somehow.

He sat down on the kerb, and looked at the Princess in despair. 'I've lost it!' he said.

'Lost what?'

'The mirror! It's the only way through I know, and it's gone. We'll never get there now!'

'Do you mean this?' Plumpearl said, taking the mirror from her purse. 'I'm sorry, I should have given it to you. I found it on the floor of the shelter this morning. You were asleep so I . . .'

'Give it to me!' shouted Andrew. 'Quick! Before they are out of sight!'

He grabbed hold of Plumpearl, and pulled her close beside him; then with his free hand, held the mirror up.

By now, the donkeys were a good way off, but he could still see them. With his heart thumping heavily, he gazed through the pale glass, terrified that this time for some reason, it would not work. But sure enough, after a few panic-stricken moments, everything surrounding them – the tree-lined avenue, the pavement under their feet – faded slowly, and a different landscape appeared instead.

In place of the avenue was a grassy track, with bushes and trees on either side; and a good way off, moving at a slow leisurely pace, they saw at once the long line of donkeys, with the miners beside them.

'MAGGINS!' yelled Andrew at the top of his voice. 'MAGGINS! – Wait!'

Calling his name, they ran after him. The procession halted, and in a moment, there was Maggins rubbing his chin, his bright blue eyes shining in his cheerful grimy face, his miners crowding round, smiling and murmuring shyly.

'Where have you sprung from?' Maggins said putting down his shovel. 'Where have you been?' This was difficult to answer in so many words.

'We – we – just sort of caught you up!' Andrew said rather lamely.

'Good job you wasn't caught by nothing else. I was worried about you – going off like that! Where did you get to?' Andrew hesitated.

'Well,' he said, 'er – you see . . .' Maggins interrupted him.

'We had a little bit of excitement you know!' He took off his cap, and pointed to the rough bandage round his head. 'Wolves! We had quite a job with them! A whole pack!'

'Yes, we saw the wolves,' Andrew said.

'Led us quite a dance!' Maggins grinned at them. 'Still, it takes more than a few wolves to stop old Maggins! I lost one of my men though.'

'He's at the Black Dragon King's Castle!' Andrew wondered as he said it how much he should tell Maggins.

'How the devil did you know that?' Maggins looked from one face to the other, at Plumpearl and back to Andrew, as he described their adventures; the encounter with the wolves, how they had stumbled on the Dragon King's stronghold and what they had overheard there. That they had been lost in the forest, but had somehow managed to find the right track; Andrew didn't mention anything else. He didn't know how to explain it.

Maggins stared at them gravely. 'I reckon you're lucky to be alive!' he said at last. 'Very lucky. I don't know what's come over those Dragon People; they're quite changed.' He coughed, looked at his feet, and then sideways at the Princess's golden clothes. There was no rough green cloak to hide them now. 'I didn't realise Ma'am, that . . . well – I thought my miners was having a joke with me! I didn't know who we had travelling with us!' He took off his cap with a flourish, and bowed before Plumpearl, smiling broadly. The other miners did the same. 'We'll get you to Kon, Ma'am, if it kills us. Won't we boys?'

'Aye! That's right!' chorused the others; and they crowded round, smiling and talking, eager to have a look at the Princess.

'And you – have you found your grandmother yet?' Maggins enquired suddenly, turning to Andrew. Andrew shook his head.

'You will. She's probably at Kon. It's the safest place these days.'

I wonder what makes him think she is in a safe place, thought Andrew wearily. He seems to take it for granted; well, I hope he's right. He sighed; he felt terribly thirsty, and his headache was worse.

'What are you sighing about?' Maggins said, laughing. 'The Hero of the day!'

'I'm all right, just tired,' Andrew said, stifling a yawn.

'You ride with me in the front then; and the Princess can sit with Oddings there behind.' He gave Andrew a leg up on to the leading donkey, and smiled up at him. 'You've done very well to get across the forest alone. There's not many grown men who could have managed it, I can tell you that.'

'I'm a bit thirsty,' Andrew muttered, 'and so is . . .'

'Yes, yes, of course. Stupid of me not to think of it. Try this! Fresh spring water is wonderfully reviving!' And he gave Andrew and Plumpearl his leather water bottle to share.

'Now – we'd best be on our way. It's only a few miles to go. We are almost there!' Maggins took the reins of the leading donkey, picked up his shovel, and the long line began to move slowly forward once more.

Andrew felt refreshed by the water, and greatly relieved that they had met Maggins again; it seemed as if they were almost at the end of their journey. At the same time, he couldn't help wondering if he was any nearer to finding his grandmother – or Miss Shooter for that matter.

9   The End of the Journey

After about three miles, sunlight began to appear between the trees ahead, and to his delight, Andrew saw that at last they were approaching the final edge of the forest.

But here a surprise awaited them. As they were about to emerge from the trees, who should step out into their path, but a small band of the Green Man's Foresters, some of whom Andrew recognised. Their leader saluted them, hailed Maggins as an old friend, and then spoke as follows, 'We feared that you had taken another path, or that we were too late!'

'Too late – for what?' Maggins enquired.

'Our Master, the Green Man, has sent us to warn you! The Black Dragon King and his men are in the valley down there' – the Forester pointed at the sunlit slopes ahead of them. 'We think they are waiting for you!'

'Is it our gold they want?' Maggins asked.

'No – the Princess of Kon, whom I believe you have travelling with you.'

'Well, they shan't have her – not if old Maggins can prevent it.' He stroked his bristly chin, and gazed towards the forest's edge.

How did they know, Andrew wondered; or is it chance? No, it can't be. Somehow they had found out – or is the Greyling down there with them? Maggins's voice interrupted his thoughts.

'What's to be done, friend? Is there another road we can take?'

'Come with us!' The Forester replied at once, 'and we will show you how best to avoid them; but the sooner we move from here the better. They may send up soldiers to search for you!'

They turned, and followed the Forester and his companions eastwards for perhaps a quarter of a mile; then cautiously approached the edge of the forest once more. Immediately ahead, the track led forward along the top of a narrow valley, which lay below them, a good way over to the left. Beyond, the ground levelled out into a featureless plain, extending for some three miles or so. In the centre of this, rising majestically towards the cloudless sky, its upper turrets and spires gleaming in the sun, stood the immense Palace he had caught a glimpse of the previous day.

Andrew stood spellbound. He couldn't believe it, they had actually found the Palace of Kon at last! Down the path, across the plain, and they were there. But what about the danger lurking below, which momentarily he had forgotten? He glanced at Maggins, who stood beside him, staring down at the bushes which covered the sides and floor of the little valley.

'You've got sharp eyes, boy,' he murmured. 'Take a look down there. Do you see anything?'

Screwing up his eyes – the sun was very bright – Andrew studied the valley beneath them. He could see the path clearly; winding between bushes and scrub, and then climbing up on the far side, and disappearing into nothingness on the sandy plain beyond. The bushes nearest to them – was there anything hiding in them? They were small thorn bushes, without many leaves, the twigs dense and black in the strong light. Suddenly he caught his breath. Something had moved behind or near

110

the one he was looking at, and he had seen the flash of sunlight on – what? Was it armour, or shining scales?

Maggins gazed at Andrew with round blue eyes. 'Someone's down there,' he said. 'Looks to me like men and dragons behind every bush! We'd best get moving.'

They retreated into the forest, where Plumpearl and the others waited in the shade.

'We must work fast, boys!' Maggins spoke in a low calm voice. 'Unload the donkeys as quickly as you can. But no noise, mind! It's not the gold they want, and we'll come back for it when we have taken the Princess across the plain.'

'We can remain here, until you return,' the Forester said. 'It would be no use us attempting to cross the plain, I fear. But we will guard your gold.'

'If the Dragon People venture out on to the plain, there will be a great battle,' Plumpearl said softly.

'What about this then?' Andrew held up the Golden Sword. He had been carrying it for so long, he had almost forgotten about it, and so, it seemed, had Plumpearl.

'Oh! – the Sword!'

'I thought that the Dragon People obeyed anyone who had this?'

'Not anyone,' the Forester said. 'The Emperor of Kon and a few others; the Greyling perhaps!'

'What about the Greyling?' Andrew asked quickly. 'Is he down there, do you think?'

'That I cannot say. I trust not,' the old man replied.

'Well, if he is, at least he hasn't got the Sword!' Andrew slipped it carefully into its sheath. 'That will help.'

It did not take long to unload the gold, and soon they had it stacked in a neat pile surrounded by shovels and picks. Each miner mounted a donkey, and with their hooked pikes taken from the baggage – some of them had two each – they sat silently waiting for Maggins's orders.

112

'Nobody's moved down there,' he said, shielding his eyes against the sun, 'but they will as soon as they see us. Now,' he beckoned to the Princess, 'you ride with Oddings here, he'll take good care of you; bunch up round her, boys, so they can't see her too quick. And you . . .' he grinned at Andrew, 'you ride with me in the front. You like a little bit of excitement, don't you?'

Andrew wasn't at all sure about this, but he felt reasonably safe with Maggins, and climbed up to sit in front of him. They said goodbye to the Foresters, and set off.

Instead of following the path down the steep hillside sloping away from the valley, as the Foresters had suggested, Maggins continued round the top, keeping just inside the tree-line. Andrew could see that he was planning to avoid the valley altogether, and lead them down on to the plain much further on. But in the end they were forced to leave the protection of the trees because of a line of sandstone cliffs dropping away to the plain beneath, and down which there appeared to be no path.

They halted for a moment, and looked over towards the Palace. 'If my father's soldiers knew we were here, they would come out to meet us,' murmured Plumpearl.

'We must just get down on to the plain – and then we shall do it!' Maggins turned in his saddle, and smiled at the others encouragingly. 'Right? Off we go!'

If you've ever tried moving fast over uneven sloping ground, on a smallish donkey, you will know how difficult it is. But two people on the same donkey, that's terrible; and if it hadn't been for Maggins's encircling arm about his waist, Andrew would have fallen off in a few seconds. The donkeys seemed to know that something special was expected of them, and careered down the bramble-covered hillside at a breakneck speed. They had almost reached the bottom, when there were shouts from the valley on their left.

'They've seen us!' yelled Maggins. 'Hold on! This will be the worst!'

The donkeys reached the plain in a few moments, and began to race headlong across it. In spite of himself, Andrew glanced over his shoulder, and through a cloud of dust, saw men running behind them, small squat men with what looked like chain-mail covering them from head to foot. From the rim of the valley, the first dragon rose into the air. Maggins turned in his seat, and shook his fist at them.

'There's a goodish gap!' he shouted. 'We'll do it! Keep going – and they can't touch us!' He was laughing.

They were travelling very fast, clumped together in a tight little bunch; Maggins and Andrew in the lead, the Princess and Oddings slightly to the left, the rest following close behind. Plumpearl's hair had come loose, and streamed out behind her. She sat easily on her donkey and was smiling happily. She evidently believed that they would reach the Palace.

But the donkeys had come a long way, and were tired. Little by little the gap began to close.

'Take the reins!' yelled Maggins, above the din of hooves, shouts, and the roars of the dragons behind them. Andrew did as he was told, and with his free hand Maggins drew out a broad two-edged sword, and brandished it in the air, shouting encouragement; the other miners held up their pikes. Andrew's heart was pounding, his mouth felt dry, and the dust was getting in his nose and eyes. But he held on to the reins firmly, and tried not to look behind.

Maggins seemed to be enjoying himself. 'Getting a bit close, aren't they?' he shouted, pointing upwards with his sword. Andrew glanced up, and to his horror saw, flapping along above them, an enormous black dragon, neck stretched out, mouth gaping open, its great wings

114

beating violently in the air. On its back, sat the Dragon King.

The huge creature was rapidly overtaking them. It swooped lower and lower, and the King leaned forward, and began to stretch out his arms. Andrew could see the rings glittering on his fingers.

'Watch out!' he shouted. 'He's going to try and lift her off!' But even as he spoke, the two miners on either side of Plumpearl, now directly beneath the Dragon King, jabbed upwards with their long barbed pikes. There was a thunderous roar from the dragon, and immediately it rose into the air, the pikes hanging from its belly. Maggins laughed again, and around him the miners cheered.

They were much nearer the Palace; less than half a mile. It rose before them out of the plain, a soaring mass of glittering golden towers and turrets; sheer unbroken walls, spires and ramparts.

'Close in! Close in!' shouted Maggins. 'Here's another one!' Andrew felt his grip tighten, and turning, saw the miners' leader gazing up at the sky once more, holding his sword firmly in his right hand.

But it was not just another one, as Andrew could see at a glance. High above them, but hurtling downwards at a tremendous speed, came a red dragon; and on it, his fur robes streaming out in the wind, sat none other than the Greyling himself.

'Look! The Greyling! – on *my dragon*!' screamed Plumpearl; and indeed the bulging eyes, and brick-red horny skin were now plain for all to see.

Afterwards, Andrew remembered thinking vaguely that the Greyling must have got in to Verbena Lodge, found the dragon, and guessed that they had been making for Kon on foot. What could they do now? – He'd beaten them. Anger seized him suddenly, and he pulled the Golden Sword from its scabbard. Perhaps it works on dragons as well as Dragon People, he thought; and he held it up pointing straight at the red dragon.

'Go back! Go back!' he shouted several times at the top of his voice. 'Shake him off! Shake him off dragon – go on, get rid of him!' At the same time, above the rattle of donkeys' hooves, he heard the shrill blast of Plumpearl's whistle; and saw her blowing on it for all she was worth, her eyes fixed on the dragon rushing towards them.

Andrew, shaken almost to pieces by the reckless pace of the donkey beneath him, stared upwards desperately, brandishing the sword. 'Go back!' he yelled again. 'Take him away! Go on – shake him off!'

Then, when only about forty feet above them, the red dragon appeared to halt almost in mid-air, its head twisting round sharply. Abruptly it changed direction, soared upwards, looped the loop several times in a crazy sweep across the sky, and then flew rapidly to a great height.

They all saw the Greyling slip from his perch, cling for a moment to the dragon's neck, and then fall, somersaulting slowly down towards the plain behind them.

In front, the central gates in the Palace walls swung open, and an avalanche of men poured out towards them. He heard Maggins shouting, 'We've done it! We've done it!' Then the donkey seemed to collapse under them both, he fell forward, a violent blow hit him on the side of the head, and that was all. Anything else that happened, or might have happened on that flat dusty plain, within yards of the Palace, he knew nothing about.

The first thing he noticed when he came to himself, was that the noise had stopped. Then, that he was lying on grass, on what looked like a large playing field in the middle of an open space or common. Someone, a man, was supporting his head, and talking to him. Everything reeled about him in awful dizzying circles, and Andrew shut his eyes.

'All right, Sonny. Take it easy! You've had a nasty fall. What's your name?'

He turned his head, and with difficulty, opened his eyes again. It took him a little while to focus properly, but when he did, he saw a man's face smiling down at him, and several other people bending over him, every expression of concern on their faces.

'I don't think you should move him,' one murmured.

'How do you feel, Sonny?' the man said again.

'Oh – not too bad. My leg hurts.'

'You really came a cropper. What's your name?'

It seemed rather silly, but for a moment, Andrew couldn't for the life of him remember; and anyway it didn't seem terribly important. He gazed up at the circle of faces, and then sat up.

'Where's Maggins – and the others? What's happened?'

He tried to hobble to his feet, and fell forward on to his knees, as an agonising pain shot up his leg. But he had time to see that beyond the little group of people who surrounded him, the flat land reared up sharply into a green ridge; and on the top of this stood an ugly brick building, complicated, high, with many roofs and turrets at different levels. Beyond this again, was more flat land.

'Oh I see – I'm – here again?' he said weakly. 'My name is – Andrew – I think!' He felt in his pocket for the mirror, found it, and took it out. The glass was cracked in several places, and fell on to the grass the moment he held it up. Somehow he had got back without it.

'I'm afraid it's broken,' the man kneeling beside him said. Andrew smiled.

'It doesn't matter – as long as I'm back. Where is this?'

'This is High Woods Common. You've had a bad fall. Where on earth were you all going on those donkeys?'

'The great Palace of Kon,' Andrew murmured, sinking down on to the grass.

'You were careering along at such a speed! I've never seen donkeys move so fast. The man in charge ought to have had more sense! Anyway they've disappeared now.'

'Probably making for Ottram,' someone suggested. 'There's a fair on in the village this afternoon.'

'What about that leg?' the man beside him said. 'Can you stand on it?'

They helped him to his feet, but he almost fell again when he tried putting his full weight on both legs. Somebody suggested that a doctor be called, or the local hospital. But in the end, they picked him up and carried him to a small house on the edge of the Common.

Andrew lay on the sofa, in the front room, feeling strangely peaceful and unconcerned about what should happen next.

'Where do you live, Sonny? Are you on the telephone?'

'I'm staying with my grandmother.' He gave them the address.

'But that's thirty miles away! What were you doing . . .?'

'I don't know,' he said. 'I really don't know what I was doing.'

Behind him someone murmured, 'Poor kid, he's concussed. Better telephone his grandmother, and then the doctor at once.' Andrew closed his eyes.

'She's not there, you won't find her. She hasn't been there for several days.'

'He's definitely rambling,' the same voice behind him said. 'Well, of course, it was an awful fall!'

Yes, he thought, it was. But not as bad as . . . as . . . that other fall. He remembered the little figure plummeting down through the bright sky. Nobody could have survived that; not even the Greyling. He wondered what the Princess was doing now – and Maggins and the rest of them? He would like to have seen the inside of that wonderful Palace. But at least they had actually got there. He was sure of that. And the Greyling was dead. He was certain of that too. He held up his hand to shield himself from the sun that was pouring in through the window, and noticed that the ring on his thumb was nothing more now than a dried up little twist of grass. He wouldn't be able to return it. Never mind, he had the strongest feeling that he no longer needed the Green Man's help.

The owner of the house came back into the room. 'I have 'phoned your grandmother,' he said. 'There seems to be a bit of trouble going on. It was a bad line, and I couldn't quite make it out. She has been away for a day or two apparently, and it seems the house has been burgled or something!'

'What?' Andrew sat up. 'She's there? My grandmother? Are you sure?'

'Quite sure. I've just spoken to her!'

'Oh! – well, I must get back at once then, or she'll worry about me!'

Joy flooded through him. Everything was all right. He *had* managed it somehow. The evil power of the Greyling was finished, broken. He jumped off the sofa where he was lying took a couple of steps across the room, gasped at the pain as his leg crumpled under him, and fell full length on the floor.

When he came to himself for the second time, he was on the big chesterfield in the drawing-room at Verbena Lodge, tucked up in one of his grandmother's travelling rugs. All round him the room was in chaos; books on the floor, curtains half down, the drawers of the desk still spilling out their contents. But – the fire was lit, the clocks on the mantelpiece ticked away merrily, and best of all, comfortably ensconced in the armchair beside him, sat Mrs Jamieson knitting and reading at the same time. He could see from where he was lying that it was a quarter to nine – but whether evening or morning he hadn't the slightest idea.

'What day is it Gran?' he asked suddenly.

'Oh hello!' His grandmother turned towards him and smiled. 'I thought that injection had put you to sleep for ever! It's still Saturday. How do you feel?'

'Fine!' He wriggled the toes of one foot, which in spite of the rug over him felt ice-cold.

'Don't try and get off there dear. You've broken your leg – and it's in plaster. Rather annoying, but you'll be able to hobble about in a day or two. And you can draw pictures on it! That's always amusing!'

'Are you a good boy?' enquired a harsh voice from the corner of the room.

'Oh that parrot!' exclaimed Mrs Jamieson. 'Frightful

Fowl, isn't in it. I don't know what's come over him! He is so contrary! I can't get him *out* of his cage now!'

Andrew struggled into a sitting position. Mrs Jamieson looked exactly the same. A little pale perhaps, but otherwise unchanged.

'Gran!' he said. 'Are you all right? What happened – to you, I mean? Where have you been?'

His grandmother put down her knitting, and sighed. 'I *am* sorry Andrew. I don't know what your parents will think – probably never trust me with you again!' She paused, frowning. 'It would be ridiculous, if it wasn't so . . .!' she hesitated, searching for the words.

'What happened to you? I've been trying to find you!'

'On High Woods Common, Andrew?'

'That's right! We'd almost got there when . . .' How could he possibly explain what he had been doing at High Woods Common? 'Tell me where you've been,' he said.

Mrs Jamieson pulled the rug up under his chin. 'Are you warm enough? she said. 'Well, you remember when Miss Shooter did not return home – on Tuesday evening, wasn't it? – Mr Grottel came to the door.'

'And he kidnapped you did he?' Mrs Jamieson stared at him.

'That's a very good guess! – Or has someone told you?' Andrew shook his head.

'Did he get hold of Miss Shooter too?'

'Well yes, actually he did! When he came to my front door, he told me that she had fainted, outside his shop; he had taken her in, and she was there resting! So of course I went round with him.'

'Was she there?' Andrew asked quickly.

'Yes she was; and believe it or not, he had told her the same story – that I had fainted, and would she come in and attend to me!'

'Have you been at Mr Grottel's then?'

'Yes! It's incredible, isn't it? He just bolted the door, and kept us there. He left us water and food; but all the same, it wasn't very comfortable! Of course when they catch him, the poor man will have to be locked up himself. I was very cross at the time; but now I feel quite sorry for him.'

Andrew thought of Plumpearl as she had been in the cage; and what would have happened if they had not managed to outwit Mr Grottel and the Greyling. And what would have become of his grandmother, Miss Shooter, and himself?

'I don't feel a bit sorry for him,' he said. 'He deserves anything he gets.'

'Andrew dear!' Mrs Jamieson turned to him with an anxious face. 'Is your leg paining you?' He shook his head.

'What happened then?'

'Well – as I say – he bolted the door and kept us there. He wouldn't listen to anything I said. He wanted the key of the Dragon Clock, but of course I hadn't got it on me!'

'No – I had it!' He felt in his pocket, 'Although I haven't got it now.'

Mrs Jamieson put her knitting down on her knees. '*You* had it! That explains it then. He kept going back to Verbena Lodge to look for it, or so he said!' A sudden thought struck Andrew.

'Were you there all the time – at Mr Grottel's?' Mrs Jamieson nodded. 'But Gran – I searched the whole house!'

'Mr Grottel's house? You couldn't have searched it quite all dear. We were there the whole time. It was odd though,' and his grandmother sounded very puzzled, 'I could never work out exactly whereabouts in the house the room was. Somewhere upstairs of course, but when we looked out of the window, there was nothing but . . .' she hesitated again.

'— trees?' prompted Andrew.

'That's right. Masses of them. Almost like a . . . a . . .'

'— forest?'

'Yes! Exactly. It was as if one was looking out at a forest. It must have been some odd view of the park, I suppose – although I should have thought it was too far away.'

Andrew was silent. It all fitted together. He understood now why those rooms had been empty. Sometimes there were traces of one world in the other – like the time he had recognised Maggins – sometimes not. There had been no traces in those empty rooms, Mr Grottel had somehow made sure of that. He, Andrew, had searched them in the ordinary everyday world; the world that he and his grandmother, and everyone else they knew, occupied every day. But she hadn't been in it! She, too, had been transported to that strange Kingdom from which he had just come. But she didn't know where she had been, or even that she had been there at all.

'So all this,' he said finally, waving his hand at the chaotic mess around them, 'was to find the key, was it?'

'Goodness knows,' sighed his grandmother. 'Of course he took the Dragon Clock – although he must have had someone with him to carry a huge thing like that; but I think it was mainly the key he wanted.'

For a moment a vision of the golden Palace of Kon, with its shining walls and towers came before his eyes. Plumpearl was there somewhere; and he was sure that the Clock and its key were there, too. It was strange after all that had happened, but he didn't really want to see her now. He was content in the knowledge that at last she was with her family, safe and happy; and the power of the Greyling was broken.

'You should see the kitchen,' Mrs Jamieson continued. 'They opened tins of this and that; made themselves a meal. Or was that you? Egg all over the place!'

'I had to eat something! It's lucky I didn't bump into him, or he would have locked me up too!'

'Andrew – where *did* you get to? Why didn't you ring someone up? Uncle David, or – well, the police?'

'It didn't occur to me,' Andrew said truthfully. He lay back on the pillows, thinking about Mr Grottel. 'How did you get out in the end? I suppose he came and unlocked the door?'

'No! Nothing of the kind. It was extraordinary. We hadn't heard anything from him for some time, since the previous day in fact; then, at about noon today, suddenly, without any warning, the whole house shook – as if we were having a minor earth tremor. It's almost unheard of in this part of the world, but it can happen. The whole room really moved before our eyes; there was dust everywhere! Quite like the time I was in Hong Kong with your grandfather.'

'Yes?'

'— Er, where was I?'

'Telling me how you got out . . .'

'Oh yes! Miss Shooter was quite alarmed. So we went to the door, and tried it once more, and it opened – easily! It was still locked but the tremor seemed somehow to have altered the shape of the doorway. Anyway, we just walked down the stairs, and straight out of the house!'

'Mm!' Andrew looked at his grandmother thoughtfully. It must have been around twelve o'clock when they were galloping towards the golden Palace of Kon, and the Greyling had fallen out of the sky on to the plain behind them.

'As we came into the hall here,' Mrs Jamieson continued, 'the telephone was ringing – to tell us that you had been found on High Woods Common with a broken leg! Andrew, what on earth were you doing on High Woods Common?'

'Looking for you! By the way, Gran – did you find

anything . . . anything else . . . in the kitchen?' He had suddenly remembered the dragon! How had it got out?

'Only a dreadful mess! There must have been more than two, actually, when I think about it; and they broke the kitchen window getting in or out!'

'Out,' murmured Andrew, 'probably,' he added, as he saw a questioning look come into his grandmother's eyes.

'I expect so. The window and its frame are completely smashed.'

He wondered if Mr Grottel or the Greyling had found the dragon asleep on the kitchen floor. Or whether they had discovered him making his own way back to Kon. The idea of that huge creature climbing up on to the kitchen sink, and bursting straight through the window, and out across Verbena Gardens struck him somehow as terribly funny, and he began to laugh.

'It's no joke,' Mrs Jamieson said. 'It'll cost pounds!'

'Hello Darling!' Scratchit flew down to perch on the end of his couch.

'Anyway, Scratchit's all right!' His grandmother took up her knitting. 'Although he could easily have got out through that hole in the kitchen. His cage has been open all this time!'

That's where he got in I suppose, thought Andrew. Aloud he said, 'What about Mr Grottel? Where's he?'

'Disappeared completely!' Mrs Jamieson said. 'The scoundrel. But I suppose they'll find him!'

But Mr Grottel was never found. It seemed as if he had disappeared off the face of the earth, which is probably what did happen to him. There were many enquiries, but neither he nor the Dragon Clock was ever seen again. His house remained empty, and then fell into disrepair; eventually it was pulled down, and some garages put up there instead. But before this happened, there was an auction of the contents of the house, and most of Mr Grottel's strange possessions were sold.

By chance, Andrew happened to be staying at Verbena Lodge, and he and his grandmother decided to go.

Lot by lot, all the things he knew so well, the piles of amber beads, the books and furniture, the thousands of clocks, the masks and tricks, were held up before the crowd, and sold for a few pounds. As far as he could remember, only the puzzle mirror, into which he had once looked, and the Vanishing Trick were missing.

Towards the end, the auctioneer held up a painting. 'And who wants this?' he called, 'this delightful painting? Not of any great value, but charming all the same.' He turned it over – 'Entitled "Parrot Boy" – what am I bid?'

'But it's exactly like you and Scratchit!' whispered Mrs Jamieson to Andrew. 'It could *be* you! What an extraordinary likeness!' – and she bought it for five pounds.

It hangs upstairs on the landing at Verbena Lodge to this day; and if you look at it carefully, very carefully, you will see that behind the boy and his parrot – who are remarkably like Andrew and Scratchit a year or two ago – in the dark and somewhat indistinctly painted background, there is a clock hanging on the wall. A large ornamental lacquered clock, with the hands set at twelve, and two carved red dragons crouching on either side of the gilded face. But no one has ever noticed this, except for Andrew. He saw it at once, of course.

More Beaver Books

We hope you have enjoyed this Beaver Book. Here are some of the other titles:

The Mill House Cat   A Beaver original. A delightful story about the adventures of Gladys and her friend Oswald, a most unusual cat! Written and illustrated by Marjorie-Ann Watts for readers of eight to twelve

Explore a Castle   An exciting and original book which helps readers to work out how castles functioned and how people lived in them, including a special section on making a model castle of your own. Written by Brian Davison and illustrated throughout with black and white photographs and line drawings

The Magicians of Caprona   Everyone in Caprona can do magic except young Tonino. But when the whole city is threatened with destruction and even Chrestomanci, the most powerful enchanter in the world, is powerless to help, it is Tonino who seems most likely to save the day! A brilliant and funny fantasy for readers of ten and over by Diana Wynne Jones

These and many other Beavers are available from your local bookshop or newsagent, or can be ordered direct from: Hamlyn Paperback Cash Sales, PO Box 11, Falmouth, Cornwall TR10 9EN. Send a cheque or postal order for the price of the book plus postage at the following rates:
UK: 45p for the first book, 20p for the second book and 14p for each additional book ordered to a maximum charge of £1.63;
BFPO and Eire: 45p for the first book, 20p for the second book, plus 14p per copy for the next 7 books and thereafter 8p per book;
OVERSEAS: 75p for the first book and 21p for each extra book.

New Beavers are published every month and if you would like the *Beaver Bulletin*, a newsletter which tells you about new books and gives a complete list of titles and prices, send a large stamped addressed envelope to:

Beaver Bulletin
Arrow Books Limited
17-21 Conway Street
London W1P 6JD

9338203